W9-BXU-917

Lightning

Also by Jean Echenoz from The New Press

Big Blondes
I'm Gone
Piano
Ravel
Running

Lightning

A Novel

Jean Echenoz

Translated from the French
by Linda Coverdale

THE NEW PRESS

NEW YORK
LONDON

The New Press gratefully acknowledges the Florence Gould Foundation
for supporting publication of this book.

The author would like to thank Margaret Cheney
(author of *Tesla: Man Out of Time*) and Mark Polizzotti.

Originally published in France as *Des éclairs* by Les Éditions de Minuit, Paris, 2010
Published in the United States by The New Press, New York, 2011
Distributed by Perseus Distribution

Library of Congress Cataloging-in-Publication Data
Echenoz, Jean.
[Des éclairs. English]
Lightning: a novel / Jean Echenoz ; translated from the French by
Linda Coverdale.
p.   cm.
ISBN 978-1-59558-649-0 (alk. paper)
I. Coverdale, Linda.   II. Title.
PQ2665.C5D4713 2011
843'.914—dc22   2011001157

The New Press was established in 1990 as a not-for-profit alternative to the
large, commercial publishing houses currently dominating the book publishing
industry. The New Press operates in the public interest rather than for private
gain, and is committed to publishing, in innovative ways, works of educational,
cultural, and community value that are often deemed insufficiently profitable.

www.thenewpress.com

Composition by dix!
This book was set in Centaur MT

Printed in the United States of America

2   4   6   8   10   9   7   5   3   1

Lightning

I

WE ALL LIKE TO KNOW, if possible, exactly when we were born. We prefer to be aware of the numerical moment when it all takes off, when the business begins with air, light, perspective, the nights and the heartbreaks, the pleasures and the days. This already provides a first landmark, an inscription, a useful number for birthdays. It also offers the point of departure for a little personal idea of time, the importance of which we all know as well, for most of us decide—agree—to wear it constantly on our person, cut up into more or less legible and sometimes even fluorescent numerals, attached by a band to our wrists, the left one more often than the right.

Well, that precise moment is something Gregor will never find out, born as he was between eleven at night and one in the morning. Midnight on the dot or a bit earlier, a bit later—no one will be able to tell him. So throughout his life he will never be sure on which day, the one before or the one after, he has the right to celebrate his birthday. He will therefore make this question of time, albeit so communal, his very first personal concern. That no one can tell him the exact hour when he appeared, however, is because this event occurred in chaotic conditions.

First of all, a few minutes before he wriggles out of his mother and while everyone is rushing around in the big house—the family shouting, footmen bumping into one another, servant girls scurrying, midwives arguing, the mother-to-be moaning—a most violent storm arises. Muttering imperiously as if to impose silence, heavy hail creates a steady, muffled din distorted by slashing gusts of wind. Then and above all, a penetrating blast of overwhelming force attempts to blow down that house. It fails, but, battering through the wide-eyed windows whose panes explode as their wooden frames begin banging back and forth, with the curtains soaring up to the ceiling or sucked outdoors, the tempest takes over the premises to destroy whatever's inside and allow rain to flood in. This wind tosses everything around, tips over furniture as it lifts up the rugs, shatters and scatters the knick-knacks on the mantelpieces, sets the crucifixes and sconces spinning on the walls, while the landscapes flip upside down and the full-length portraits go ass over teakettle. Turning the chandeliers into swings, instantly snuffing their candles, the gale blows out all the lamps as well.

Gregor's birth proceeds like this in the clamorous darkness

until a gigantic lightning bolt—thick, branching, a grim pillar of burnt air shaped like a tree, like its roots or the claws of a raptor—spotlights his arrival and sets the surrounding forest on fire, while thunder drowns out his first cry. Such is the bedlam that in the general panic, no one takes advantage of the frozen glare of the flash, its instant broad daylight, to check the precise time according to clocks that, cherishing long-standing differences, have disagreed among themselves for quite a while anyway.

A birth outside of time, therefore, and out of the light, because in those days the only illumination comes from candle wax and oil, since electric current is as yet unknown. Electricity—as we employ it today—has yet to impose itself on custom, and it's about time for someone to deal with that. It's Gregor who'll take charge, as if sorting out another item of personal business: it will be his job to clear the matter up.

2

Since coming into the world that way might make anyone a tad high-strung, Gregor's character declares itself early on: stormy, contemptuous, touchy, abrupt, he turns out to be precociously unpleasant. He quickly acquires a reputation for capriciousness, temper tantrums, stubborn silences, inopportune mischief and escapades, breaking things, sabotage, and other destructive behavior. In that vein, doubtless wishing to settle the question of time, which seems so close to his heart, as soon as he is able he begins taking apart all the clocks and watches in the house—so he can try to put them back together, naturally, he then discovers, not a little furious, that the first stage of the operation always goes smoothly, whereas success in the second stage proves much more elusive.

Gregor also appears, however, to be extremely impressionable, nervous, fragile, and especially—even abnormally—sensitive to sound. All kinds of noises, rumbles, vibrations, and echoes bother him excessively even if they're quite far away, imperceptible to anyone else, and such sounds can pitch him into frightening rages. He is also subject to serious fits during which he re-experiences, even beneath a placid sky, the lightning flash of his birth and seems dazzled to the point of blindness, panicking his family and perplexing every hastily summoned doctor. To top off this anarchic situation, Gregor grows unusually rapidly: he becomes very tall very fast, and even faster, taller than everyone else.

This troubled childhood unfolds somewhere in south-eastern Europe, far from everything except the Adriatic, in an isolated village wedged between two mountain ranges and without access to any possible healers of the soul. There Gregor can sometimes calm himself only by spending hours contemplating birds. Yet though his turbulent character at first provokes fears of eventual madness, those close to him must admit that his intelligence is growing even more swiftly than his lanky frame.

Having for instance learned a good half-dozen languages in five minutes, casually completed his youthful schooling by skipping half the grades, and above all, put paid to that problem with the clocks—which he soon manages to dismantle and reassemble in an instant, blindfolded, leaving them all forever exact to the nanosecond—Gregor becomes the prize student at the first polytechnic university that comes along. There, far from his village, he absorbs in a flash mathematics, physics, mechanics, and chemistry, subjects that now allow him to think up inventions of all kinds, and with singular skill. His memory is as precise as the recently discovered process of photography. In fact Gregor is particularly gifted at being able to imagine things as if they already existed, seeing them with such three-dimensional accuracy that to design the workings of his creations, he almost never needs sketches, diagrams, models, or preliminary experiments. Since he immediately considers anything he imagines as *true*, the only risk he runs, and will perhaps always run, is that of confusing what he's conceptualizing with reality.

And since he has no time to lose, the devices he envisions have nothing about them of the trivial, the accessory, the piddling detail. Gregor will never be the type to perfect a lock, improve a can opener, or tinker with a gas lighter. When ideas come to him, they're clearly of a high order—very high—in cosmic import and universal interest.

For example, one of his first inspirations is to install a tube at the bottom of the Atlantic that would allow, among other things, the rapid exchange of mail between Europe and America. Gregor's initial design involves a pumping system to send pressurized water through the conduit to propel spheres containing such correspondence along their way, but the drag created by this water rubbing against the inside of the tube is too powerful, so Gregor abandons this project in favor of an equally ambitious one.

Now it's a question of building a gigantic ring up above and encircling the equator. At first turning freely at the same speed as our planet, it would then be immobilized by a re-actionary force so that we could all go inside it and circle the earth at about one thousand miles an hour—although in reality, the *earth* would be whirling beneath *us* as we admire the view, comfortably seated in armchairs (the ergonomic design of which Gregor has offhandedly but precisely anticipated), going "around the world" in a day.

Obviously, these are not small-minded undertakings, for Gregor is bent upon confronting challenges of vast dimensions. Early on, along those lines, he becomes convinced he'd like to do a little something with tidal power, tectonic movements, or solar energy, phenomena like that, or—why not?—just to get his hand in, the falls at Niagara. He's seen engravings of them in books and feels they'll fit the bill. Yes, Niagara Falls. The Niagara River would be good.

In the meantime, with his diplomas stuffed into his pockets, Gregor heads off to work in a few great cities of western Europe where his abilities, he has been assured, will find more fertile ground for rapid development. There he finds varied employment as an engineer, expert, or consultant, but he is still unsatisfied. To occupy himself outside of office hours, he builds his first serious machine. It's a new kind of alternating current induction motor, which he shows with his usual arrogance to his colleagues, who at first look way down their noses at it. Then, having drained the cup of jealousy to its dregs, forced to admit that this apparatus could change everything, his colleagues set aside their irritation and take it upon themselves to suggest to Gregor that he should perhaps head even farther west, where even more rich and fertile ground ought to allow his ideas to fully flower and bear fruit. It's possible that this advice is not entirely disinterested and that these colleagues would like to get rid of Gregor because, not content with being unpleasant, he's beginning to be somewhat in the way.

And besides, although he's beyond the age when growing runs out of steam, Gregor is still getting taller.

3

So at twenty-eight, now just over six and a half feet tall, Gregor sails off to the United States of America. He disembarks on a dock in New York equipped with his passport and bowler hat, a small suitcase containing a very few personal effects, another one containing a very few tools, twenty dollars folded into a pocket, and, safe in a different pocket, a letter of recommendation addressed to Thomas Edison.

Edison is a wealthy and powerful inventor, the founder of the Edison Electric Company, who is so famous at this point that, while still alive and kicking, he has already appeared as a central character in a novel by the French symbolist Villiers de L'Isle-Adam that was recently serialized in the review *La Vie moderne*. Credited with more than 1,093 inventions (many the work of others, which he boldly adds to his own), Edison claims in particular to have invented the telephone, motion pictures, and sound recording, not to mention electricity, on which we're going to spend quite a bit of time here.

Having first thought up—after many other things—the incandescent light bulb, Thomas Edison has perfected a distribution system to supply those light bulbs, and two years later, he inaugurates the first electrical powerhouse in the world. When Gregor arrives, it is already furnishing 110-volt continuous current to fifty-nine families living in Manhattan within the immediate periphery of Edison's laboratory. The inventor considers this only a beginning, however: he has just improved the system by creating a network serving various factories and plants, as well as some theaters scattered around New York City. The enterprise is ripe for continued growth, but requires more capital, more investment. Well, financiers don't yet seem fully able to grasp all the advantages of this electricity—except for the richest financier of all, a certain John Pierpont Morgan. A formidable man, feared for his power and nasty character, John Pierpont Morgan is also held in awe for his shrewdness and foresight: preferring to say nothing and bide his time, he has immediately understood that this new energy is the best discovery in the whole history of science since Archimedes invented the screw.

In spite of his excessive height, Gregor is handsome, slender, distinguished, self-assured; his long face sports an elegant mustache, but he feels rather intimidated at his first meeting with Edison, even though the inventor isn't much to look at—and perhaps precisely because of that. Edison is an ugly man with shifty eyes, stooped, gauche, and disagreeable, who drags his feet when he walks and always wears the vaguely beige or brownish cotton lab coats his wife sews for him buttoned up to his chin. He's deaf, by the way, thanks to a stubborn bout of scarlet fever when he was thirteen, a handicap that didn't prevent him from imagining and constructing, seventeen years later, the first phonograph.

What's more, when Gregor shows up at his house, Edison is in a foul mood: for the past few days, there have been increasing problems with his continuous-current installations at various businesses or private homes. And while his engineers are all off dealing with emergency repairs at the Fifth Avenue home of the Vanderbilts, he's just been informed that the Edison dynamos of the steamer *Oregon* have packed it in as well. With its vessel forced to remain at moorings, the shipping company is losing huge sums every day and is threatening to take action against Edison. As stingy as he is irascible, Edison has no more personnel at hand when Gregor timidly gives him his letter, which praises his talents as an electrician. Just on the off chance, without any hope or even a glance at the young man, Edison sends him off on the strength of the letter to evaluate the situation aboard the *Oregon*.

Gregor has a little trouble finding out where the harbor is, and then the dock where the steamer is moored. His eye is caught by seagulls soaring overhead. He has always been captivated by flying things, and in particular—go figure—by pigeons, doves, turtledoves, and others of that ilk. But, well, gulls are not without interest, either. After Gregor has watched them hover and dive for a moment, a surly officer shows him the way to the engine room, where he shuts himself up alone with his instruments. Tackling the dynamos, he repairs them during the night. When Gregor returns the next morning to Edison's offices, the inventor hires him without a word as his assistant, at a bellhop's salary.

4

AN ASSISTANT, IN EDISON'S VIEW, is a drudge, a handyman rather than a trustworthy man, and Gregor's role will consist above all of obeying the most diverse commands regarding menial, even household tasks, without any particular license to have his own say. It's a steady position, though, to cope with the increasingly frequent difficulties cropping up with the equipment installed by Edison Electric. The persistence of these breakdowns finally suggests, and then reinforces some doubt in Gregor's mind regarding the very principle on which Edison's equipment is based, namely, continuous current.

Let's try to understand it, this continuous current. It's a current, meaning a flow of electricity, you see, in which the electrons constantly go in only one direction. Its dynamos produce rather weak voltage, which must be compensated for by greater strength. Thus the necessity of using thick cables, which can lead to great losses, since the resistance of said cables transforms part of the current into heat. Now, heat can quickly lead to sparks, conflagration, disaster, firemen and insurance investigators, all very annoying. Besides, continuous current cannot be carried for more than about two miles in these cables, which are not capable of withstanding the high tensions required for distant transmissions. Customers must therefore live, like Edison's neighbors, close to a power station to receive any electricity. The result is a system plagued by important malfunctions: chronic breakdowns, frequent accidents, and periodic fires; lawsuits, trials, damages. Thomas Edison can say what he likes, but something is wrong.

During his studies, Gregor had definitely noticed that something was wrong when his physics teacher showed him a machine of the same type as Edison's that was throwing off way too many sparks. Gregor had timidly suggested replacing the continuous current with an alternating current, meaning one that reverses direction at regular intervals. Wouldn't that work better? The instructor had shrugged and opined that such an idea smacked of perpetual motion, and therefore impossibility, so Gregor hadn't pressed his point.

Now that he's working at Edison Electric, Gregor has mentioned this hypothesis concerning alternating current once or twice, but since Edison explodes each time as if his assistant were extolling the Antichrist, Gregor has still not pressed his point.

But he has impressed his boss, by solving many technical problems and working eighteen hours a day, seven days a week. Now doubt has crept into Edison's suspicious brain as well: that such a gifted and conscientious individual could mention any option other than continuous current puts him increasingly on his guard. Once Gregor has described to Edison how he might possibly improve the output of his generator, the boss tells him, Fine, go to it: there's $50,000 in it for you if you succeed. Gregor goes to it, for six months, at the end of which the generator winds up in fine fettle indeed. Gregor hurries to report to his employer.

Great, exclaims Edison, lounging in his armchair with his feet propped up on his desk. Good, very good. Really? asks Gregor uneasily. You're pleased? Ecstatic, declares Edison, delighted. So, then, ventures Gregor, unable to finish his sentence, because—So then what? breaks in Edison, whose face has turned to stone. Actually, says Gregor, screwing up his courage, I seem to remember something about $50,000. Young man, snaps Edison, sitting up and taking his feet off his desk, you mean to tell me you don't know an American joke when you hear one?

This time, Gregor stands up, heads for the coat tree to get his bowler, then to the door through which he goes without closing it behind him or saying a word, then to the bookkeeper's office to get his salary, then out to the street, wondering what he's going to do after that dirty trick.

Well, it's quite simple: he will try to develop his little theory about alternating current on his own. During the three years spent with Edison, he has quickly made a name for himself with his prompt efficiency and original solutions, so his reputation as an engineer has rapidly spread beyond the offices of the Edison Electric Company. Gregor therefore goes to see a group of financiers to whom he explains his ideas. Present state of the system; critique of the system; ways to improve it; firm estimate of time required for completion of the job; detailed budget.

Well, things work out just fine. Building on his precocious gift for languages and his already considerable knowledge of English, these first American years have allowed Gregor to swiftly master the idiom. He possesses natural eloquence, a talent for presenting his projects, and persuasive confidence, which will all continue to stand him in good stead. Discussing the matter after his departure, the businessmen agree that Gregor is definitely on to something. They ask him to return the next day and declare themselves interested enough to propose founding the Gregor Electric Light Company, in the bosom of which he will be able to pursue his research. Of course, as the backers of the firm, they will be the majority shareholders, you understand, but Gregor ought to invest some funds as well to justify the company name and his new position. Gregor allows as how that's only natural and hands over all the money he's saved in his three years at Edison Electric in one fell swoop: all of it, which is to say, not much, but still, all of it. And since all of it is not enough, what does he do but boldly borrow more.

Well, after that things move right along. In the time it takes to invent an arc lamp immediately patented, offered to consumers, and quickly lucrative, time enough for his partners to see a nice little return on their investment and a handsome profit, Gregor finds himself promptly fired from his own business, which his associates take over, happy to celebrate their success, leaving him cleaned out. That's how he winds up back in the street—a porter, an excavation laborer, an unskilled construction worker riddled with debts—for four years.

5

THAT WAS ANOTHER DIRTY TRICK, but the workmen are en-
joying their break and as at every building site, summer and
winter alike, Gregor has kept on his bowler. It's winter, as
it happens, and to warm up, we're eating some hot potatoes
and ham. The ham is wrapped in sulfurized paper on which
grease has left a stain shaped pretty much like the eastern
European region where Gregor was born, and on this stain, as
he chews, he reconstructs with strips of rind the two mountain ranges flanking his native village, indicated with a pellet
of bread. Lacking the precise date, that's how he presents his
birthplace to a foreman who has taken a kind of liking to
him—even though Gregor never lifts a finger to inspire such
sympathy.

We're sitting on crates and sacks of cement in the shadow
of some picks and shovels stuck into a pile of sand, near a fire
of plaster-spattered planks in the middle of a work site along

a major artery in Brooklyn. A chain-wire fence separates the site from the muddy and tumultuous avenue sending its noise skimming over our heads and along which hurries the dense traffic of men on horseback, pedestrians, handbarrows, horse-drawn wagons and omnibuses, all vehicles that Gregor counts carefully, albeit automatically, one after another and by categories, the way he habitually counts whatever comes his way. Also circulating on the avenue are those new electric streetcars that keep breaking down—when they're not derailing, terrorizing their passengers as well as passersby, so that everyone is complaining about them.

They'll never work, those trams, remarks the foreman sitting near Gregor. They're not suitable for city streets. Yes they are, replies Gregor. They'll wind up fitting in one of these days. It all depends on the energy system, that's what's not working—the continuous current. Just what would you know about it? asks the foreman uneasily. Well, I'm an engineer, aren't I, says Gregor stiffly, that's my real profession. Electricity.

And he begins to explain, in short, clear, and astonishingly understandable sentences, the inconveniences of continuous current, whereas an alternating system would permit the use of transformers to raise and lower the voltage. Thanks to these transformers, thousands of volts could be sent hundreds of miles, as much as you like, through high-tension lines. Low amperage would mean low leakage, you see.

At first the other man looks at him strangely, torn between the curious feeling of instantly understanding a foreign language and the suspicion that his companion is rambling, but as Gregor warms to his theme, the foreman visibly relaxes.

At the end of the line, concludes Gregor, other transformers installed in substations can step down the voltage for the customers' use. Current could in this way be distributed over great distances, eliminating the need to live near a power plant to have electricity. That's why alternating current would be better: it would cost much less and work much better. Same thing with the trams. But I'm boring you with all this.

Not at all, says the foreman, no indeed. Why? asks Gregor. You find this interesting? Not necessarily, replies the foreman, but I may know someone who will. A friend of mine.

6

THE FOREMAN'S FRIEND is basically someone who knows someone else, or rather, works for someone else, as his butler, in fact. Now, a butler, if he is a good butler, can become a trusted employee in whom one confides regarding subjects other than stewardship or household matters, someone with whom intimate sorrows, professional or conjugal, are willingly shared. And the employer of this butler just happens to hold an important position in the Western Union Telegraph Company, a firm managed by the entrepreneur George Westinghouse and—incidentally—a competitor of the Edison Electric Company.

The foreman recalls certain conversations in a bar with his butler friend during which, between two pints, the latter mentioned his employer, who over time has come to confide in him. After domestic matters have been dealt with, and suggestive sighs have alluded to the suspicions he harbors about his too-young wife, the employer has also touched upon certain issues facing Western Union, among which, in addition to problems providing gas and telephone service, figure those concerning electricity, a major preoccupation for George Westinghouse. And on this subject the foreman remembers that this "alternating current" mentioned by Gregor has definitely cropped up in those conversations. If you like, says the foreman, I can speak to my friend. What have we got to lose?

Gregor doesn't object to such an initiative. The information takes a few days to percolate up via the butler to his employer, then—who knows how—all the way to George Westinghouse himself, who lets it be known that, good heavens, he wouldn't mind learning a little more about this. In his crummy furnished apartment, Gregor, informed, finds himself in a quandary over this appointment set for later that morning. It's not himself he's worried about, but his appearance: since such a meeting demands attire more formal than work clothes, Gregor goes out to buy new celluloid cuffs and a detachable collar before shining his shoes and spending some time brushing his one suit and his bowler hat.

After an entrance hall followed by several more interminable halls decorated with chandeliers, marble, carpets, statues, paintings, tapestries, and the occasional usher, this already long traipse through the headquarters of Western Union leads to a slow tracking shot at the end of which George Westinghouse finally appears in person, installed behind a gothic desk

nd for a quarter apiece, whatever their condition.
uptible as any other kids, the children set out to
many as possible, selling them off as agreed to be
little shows.

mals end up strapped to a board in the middle of
s the crowd passes by, where, after a short presenta-
a, they are subjected by the pitchman to a goodly
of alternating current with a result you can imag-
a smoke, sparks, cracklings and clamor, smells of
sh, and cadaveric rigidity. Gawkers are deeply im-
ad now, having demonstrated the pernicious dan-
s technology, the huckster can only denounce it,
ag its dreadful effects and exhorting the populace
out of their homes.

nimals having soon been judged insufficient, the
is repeated with bigger beasts before growing
aile underlings circulate among the spectators,
g frightening pamphlets describing alternat-
, in a touch of overkill, as a mortal danger. Thus
cuted in public numerous sheep, calves, bullocks,
gor observes all this from a distance and unfazed:
artyred mammals leave him cold. As long as no
armed, it's fine. In short, Edison Electric executes
beasts, and finally makes plans to tackle a behe-
upreme animal.

would have it, an opportune occasion arises:

at the far end of a room as big as a stadium. A tall fellow, massive, a solid block, whose jowls seem to weld his head to his trunk, draped with watch chains and the swags of a walrus mustache, a man of few words. Cold blue eyes, no time to waste, plunging right in, he points to an armchair with his fat manicured hand, adorned with a signet ring of cast iron.

Sitting up stiffly on the edge of his seat, not touching the back or armrests, hands crossed on his lap, sensing that he should get straight to the point, Gregor swiftly recaps his past work—rotating magnetic field, the concept of an asynchronous motor—but only in passing, for the record, before launching into his ideas on alternating current. That is the only subject he develops, without even bothering to compare it with the continuous current system, which is Edison's exclusive property. Sticking essentially to the same presentation he gave the foreman, although savvy enough to go into more detail for an engineer, Gregor marshals his arguments and calculations so decisively that he is hired on trial, after a half-hour interview, as a consultant. Westinghouse will give him the means to develop his system: a laboratory, two assistants, necessary materials, a minimum salary, short-term results required.

Gregor leaves his job at the building site that afternoon, invites the foreman for a drink, gets to work at Westinghouse the next morning and—let's not linger here—in short order comes up with a motor, a generator, and a transformer implementing his idea. Then come technical trials and verifications, applications for patents, a nod of endorsement from Westinghouse, and the decision to construct these machines all over the place. Things seem to be working out; life, apparently, is beginning to fall into place.

Life *is* sweeter, and on some evenings, after leaving the lab, Gregor allows himself to linger a little in the public parks, especially in Reservoir Park where he buys a small bag of popcorn for himself and another of seeds to feed the pigeons. He always goes there alone because he is always alone and, unlike other men, he seems much more inclined to contemplate these birds than to admire, say, any girls.

Life will soon take an even more favorable turn when Westinghouse offers Gregor a contract with Western Union. The agreement stipulates that in addition to his salary, he will receive in royalties $2.50 per horsepower of electric power sold. That doesn't look like much, at first glance, but still, it's something. Besides, they're going to start selling now, and seriously. After its commercial inauguration, polyphase alternating current will be distributed on a grand scale to supply all of North America. One can see this is a huge undertaking. Of considerable importance. Of unprecedented design. Of enormous enterprise. All the newspapers are talking about it.

Edison reads the newspapers.

IN THE MONTHS THAT FOLLO\
and dogs, be they Siamese or\
begin to vanish with abnorn\
laboratory and offices of Edis

Edison has indeed read th\
ing some alarming rumors, h\
nopoly clearly threatened by\
alternating current, he must\
off public opinion, and try to\
nology that might well depri\
Edison has therefore devised\
one's attention.

If Edison Electric's neighb\
find their pets disappearing at\
unusual trade has sprung up i\
Edison's agents tell the local

they can\
So, as co\
capture a\
featured

The a\
the street\
tion spee\
discharg\
ine, rich\
charred\
pressed.\
gers of t\
condemn\
to keep i

Small\
experim\
crowds\
distribu\
ing curr\
are elect\
horses.\
all these\
birds ar\
ever hef\
moth, tl

As l

at Luna Park in Coney Island, in fact, an elephant has just been condemned to death. Twenty-eight-year-old Topsy has worked hard all her life in circuses and can't take being forced to do any more of those endless exercises balancing on one foot. Although they're a crowd-pleaser, they bring on terrible bouts of arthrosis that don't improve her mood, so that in a moment of pique and exasperation, she has crushed three abusive trainers. Verdict: capital punishment. Death by hanging is the initial choice (a sentence successfully carried out thirteen years later with her elephantine colleague Big Mary), but they switch to a dish of cyanide-seasoned carrots, which the wily Topsy refuses to touch. What to do? Embarrassment all around. That's when Edison offers his services.

This opportune occasion demands a grand display, however, and in particular, the perfect distribution medium. Now, along with a thousand other things, Thomas Edison has always been interested in motion pictures. Seriously litigious, by the way, he's embroiled in a war over contracts concerning that new art. He's even busy producing the first Western and gangster film in the world, *The Great Train Robbery*, in the last frame of which an outlaw shoots a conclusive bullet at the terrified audience. But at the same time as he's thus launching himself into fiction, he'll try his hand as well at the documentary.

Filmed thanks to Edison in front of 1,500 people, the elephant's electrocution will be shown throughout the country.

We can see the carefree pachyderm, watched by a delighted crowd, happily appear before the camera, merry as a lark, even though her feet and trunk are linked by cables to a generator. Topsy suspects nothing, however, because she was captured soon after her birth in a forest in Orissa, on the east coast of India, and she's used to being tethered. Then, once they've gotten her to stand still on a sheet of metal, they hit her with 6,600 volts. Thick smoke billows from the leads connected to her body, which collapses instantly like a popped balloon, a big skin sack suddenly emptied out, its sprawling legs pointing to the four points of the compass. Quod erat demonstrandum. The applause is deafening.

8

WHILE EDISON IS BEAVERING AWAY, Gregor isn't wasting a minute either. He needs to move swiftly on to something else. He shouldn't stop or even take a break by simply resting on his laurels after completing the project for Westinghouse, which was really nothing but the application of an idea conceived long ago, ten years earlier in a park in eastern Europe. Gregor has had to wait a while before making that idea a reality, but to him it's already ancient history.

So without coasting along on his new salary or pausing to see what happens, he immediately begins developing his arc lamps with several projects concerning light, and then he works—among other things—on a thermomagnetic motor, a pyromagnetic generator, and a commutator for a dynamo-electric machine. Not that he feels or finds himself constrained by anyone to produce, to find new ideas and always keep inventing, no, it's just that he can't help it, being in this regard and in his own eyes (for he holds, it must be said, a rather lofty opinion of himself) more imaginative than anyone else.

That all his inventions work the way he'd thought they would even before he'd built a single machine—the experiments always proceed according to his plans—is thanks to his singular ability to see the object with precision in his mind, in three dimensions and exquisite detail. The various parts of these devices rapidly appear to him with the utmost reality and as if tangible in all their attributes, down to the very ways in which these parts will wear out.

Such aptitudes, however—and especially this excessive intrusion of actuality into the imagination, this invasion of an idea taking itself for real—also risk cutting you off somewhat from the world, or in any case from people who deal with that material reality. Which is why, whenever Westinghouse offers assistants to Gregor, it never pans out. Supremely disdainful of their drawing boards, preferring his instantaneous interior designs, he makes life truly hard for his colleagues, inflicting his mood swings on them, reproaching and belittling them when they can't understand things fast enough, replacing them at a brisk tempo—if they don't throw their hands up first and walk out. It's soon obvious that he prefers to work alone, with no one else around except his bookkeeper.

It's also evident, by the way, that Gregor prefers to be alone and live alone in general, and to look at himself in mirrors rather than at other people, and to do without women even though they find him very attractive: he's quite handsome, quite tall, brilliant, has a way with words, he's not yet forty, and he's available. Even though he's certainly not indifferent, given that he's not any fonder of men, to the fact that women cluster discreetly around him, so far Gregor apparently prefers that they keep a certain distance. But this is in part due to various specific aspects of his personality.

A personality that is, after all, impossible, and a few of his traits—we'll mention only two—keep Gregor too busy to leave him much wiggle room. First off, his extreme preoccupation with microbes, bacilli, and all sorts of germs requires him constantly to clean every object around him well beyond reason, without ever assigning this chore to anyone else, plus he washes his hands before cleaning and again when he's done. Then there's his mania for counting everything, perpetually, which is an absorbing task as compelling as a law. He counts the paving stones of avenues, the steps of stairs, the floors of buildings, counts his own footsteps from one place to another and compares the results each time, counts passersby in the street, clouds in the sky, trees in the parks, birds in these trees as well as in the sky and among them, in particular, pigeons are counted separately.

The only thing Gregor doesn't count carefully, as if it were outside the law—thus the necessary and permanent presence of a bookkeeper—is money. Gregor hasn't the head for it.

Besides, his counting takes up even more of his time in that it's not only mechanical, but has also invaded the realm of emotions: in the infinite crowd of numbers that occupy his mind, each one inspires a particular emotion in Gregor, a special flavor, a color all its own, and nothing can rival his major affection for numbers divisible by three—a lovely number, as we know, suitable for any occasion. Anything that can be divided by three, in Gregor's eyes, is better. Nothing is more beautiful to him than a multiple of three.

9

Appearing like clockwork at every street corner before
being shown on the nation's first movie screens, the animal
electrocutions initially stir up rather strong emotions, then
continue having their little effect, of course, but perhaps these
demonstrations, even elephantine, soon lose their luster. Folks
are quickly bored; such is the fickleness of man, etc. Seeing
which, Edison and his Edison Electric begin to wonder if,
while they're at it, the application of alternating current to a
human being wouldn't be just the ticket, spectacular and to
the point, the best way to impress people and convince them
of the system's dangers. Now all they need is a volunteer.

Candidates aren't crowding around, of course, spontane-
ously eager to help out. After much research, and discreet
enquiries made in various institutions, asylums, shelters, and
clinics regarding melancholy individuals tired enough of life
to perhaps eventually be tempted by the noose, strychnine,

free falls, the trusty Colt 45, or the more recent Browning 7.65, it turns out that no one is tired enough to consider wearing electrodes. Discouragement ensues; perhaps Edison Electric should give up on the idea. And then the perfect subject finally appears on the horizon.

Imprisoned in Sing Sing, this first client is one William Kemmler, who has just somehow managed to massacre his female companion with an ax. Well, such behavior is frowned upon, and being drunk doesn't excuse a thing. Since it is not civil to hack up one's concubine like that, the accused has been condemned to death, a verdict the aforesaid Kemmler himself, quite logically, accepts.

Up until that time, in such cases, the condemned was hanged. But through connections, arguing that his new system is more humane than the brutal gallows, being quicker, more sanitary, and less painful, Edison manages to have an adequate apparatus set up in the penitentiary. Since being subjected to such treatment deserves a minimum of comfort, it's decided that the subject should be sitting down. And so an oak innocently growing in the prison courtyard is felled and chopped up to provide the wood William Kemmler's fellow prisoners slap together into a rudimentary armchair. Two electrodes inside moist sponges are attached to this chair and linked to a Westinghouse dynamo acquired on the sly. And one August morning at six o'clock, in a room paradoxically lit by gaslight and before some twenty witnesses, journalists, priests, and doctors, William Kemmler is seated in this brand-new chair.

The first attempt to execute him fails: after an electric shock of a thousand volts, administered over seventeen seconds, Kemmler is still alive. Naturally everyone would like to try again as quickly as possible, but the generator requires some time to recharge. So there's a goodly pause, an irksome interval during which Kemmler, horribly burned, can be heard screaming and moaning, which produces an excellent ambience. With the generator recharged, a second attempt takes one long minute during which the voltage is upped this time to two thousand: a strong smell of broiling flesh is quickly noted as long sparks shoot from Kemmler's limbs, his abundant sweat gradually changes to blood, a thick column of smoke rises from his head, and his eyes try successfully to escape from their sockets, at which point, attested to by a forensic pathologist, he is undoubtedly dead.

So that's done. After this first charred convict, the unfortunate effects of alternating current on human beings are henceforth undeniable. Thomas Edison is not displeased. The horror felt by all those who witnessed Kemmler's end, to which they can now attest, suits his purposes admirably, since such a system will now be forever linked to the name of Westinghouse. Let's understand his satisfaction and never forget that the most wonderful inventions often have quite wonderful histories. Because this, for example, is how the electric chair was born: as a publicity stunt.

10

Edison can beaver away all he likes, but the tides are turning in the electric war he is waging with Westinghouse. The latter, having understood the superiority of alternating current and championed its virtues among his close colleagues, now dreams of providing this new service throughout the North American continent: he is presenting his case, gaining influence, and rallying support. To assist him and counteract Edison Electric's spectacular publicity campaign, Gregor undertakes a series of lectures in the United States and then Europe.

In view of these public performances, and severely depleting—despite the frowning looks of his sharp-eyed bookkeeper—his first subsidies from Western Union, Gregor immediately acquires a new wardrobe, intent on becoming the best-dressed man on Fifth Avenue. He sticks to his strictly black suits, but refines their cut, substitutes flannel if not gabardine for their coarse cloth, switches to shirts of lawn or batiste, collects ties as well as kid, suede, and lamb-skin gloves (whose dreaded microflora will quickly instill in him the habit of never using them, as with his three daily handkerchiefs of white silk, more than once), equips himself with a bevy of canes carved from rare woods and sporting or-nate pommels, and for the finishing touch, trades in his single bowler for an army of top hats and Panamas. And yet, in spite of this foray into elegance, Gregor never wears jewelry: he has such a horror of trinkets that he never wears a chain on his watch, a pin in his tie, or the slightest ring on any finger.

During his lectures, he is of course supposed to talk up the service provided by Westinghouse, and his boss has complete confidence in Gregor. Who, however, not wishing to thus limit himself and eager to share his new ideas as well, takes advantage of this opportunity to put on a little show.

Before an audience plunged into total darkness occasion-ally streaked here and there with furtive gleams, Gregor sud-denly appears in a circle of white light as if out of nowhere dressed in his tailored black frock coat, with his long pale face and tall silhouette made even taller by a top hat, surrounded on his platform by extravagant objects, equipment never seen before: solenoidal bobbins, incandescent lamps, various coils, and above all, many glass tubes of every shape filled with gas under low pressure.

Mysterious and theatrical, carefully managing his lighting

and his effects, Gregor backs up his talents as an orator with his gifts as an actor, and his conjuring is almost magical. Since the primary object is to prove the safety of the alternating system, with one hand he picks up a wire from a coil through which runs a high-voltage current, and with the other hand, a tube—that lights right up, to the stupefaction of the audience. Gregor has thus shown that electricity, passing through his body, has not hurt him at all. Of course, to bring off this demonstration, Gregor has used a high-frequency current that cannot penetrate his body yet circulates safely on its periphery, so he's pulled a bit of a fast one with a very tiny trick, but no matter: the audience is convinced and success assured.

Having triumphantly carried out Westinghouse's instructions, however, Gregor soon begins to take a few initiatives. No longer content just to celebrate the advantages and safety of alternating current, without informing his boss he rapidly proceeds to expound on all his new ideas—in the front ranks of which figures a new concept, hitherto unheard-of, never before presented to the public: the discovery of a free, diffuse, kinetic energy that Gregor claims is available throughout the universe and which, my goodness, is just asking to be exploited. It's only a question of time, Gregor announces rashly. It won't take long, he exclaims, for humanity to bring its power technologies into harmony with the great workings of nature. Kept informed of these goings-on by his perplexed agents, stationed in the audience to monitor the situation, Westinghouse indulgently turns a blind eye.

With his dramatic presence, his mastery of expression, surprise, and suspense, backed up by his finesse and sleight of hand, Gregor immediately enjoys considerable success with his lectures and receives incredible press coverage, while word of mouth creates a momentum that increases day by day. Before long he is the only subject of conversation at fashionable dinner parties, so that—you see how all this can snowball— in a few months Gregor quite simply becomes the most famous scientist in the world.

With lightning speed, everyone begins fighting over him. He's abruptly showered with honors and decorations. Foreign governments seek out his services. He is called a magician, a visionary, a prophet, a prodigious genius, hailed as the greatest inventor of all time. Now he's courted by New York's highest society, industrialists and financiers, newspaper magnates, university presidents, writers, actors, musicians, poets, sculptors, politicians, presidents, kings, you name it.

He accepts then often declines invitations to the homes of the rich, the very rich, and the filthy rich. The fashion is for the rich to give banquets called silver, gold, diamond, or platinum dinners, the distinction among them hanging on the nature of the jewelry every lady finds as a party favor, nestled under her starched napkin, when she takes her place at the table. Gregor attends one or two of these dinners, but his distaste for jewelry is such that he stops going. The very rich do more or less the same thing at their soirées, except that all cigarettes are rolled with hundred-dollar bills—and frankly, Gregor doesn't see the point. The filthy rich are even more twisted, throwing bizarre parties where it's considered good form, for example, for multimillionaire guests to arrive unshaven, with unkempt hair, dressed in grubby rags, and sit on a dirty floor drinking flat beer while dining on scraps—crusts, pork rinds, turnip tops—served on crystal plates by bewigged and liveried footmen. Gregor doesn't show what he thinks of all this; perhaps he finds it diverting for a few minutes, but he soon stops attending these events as well.

Even though titans like Rudyard Kipling, Mark Twain, and Ignace Paderewski figure among all the celebrities he frequents, with whom he could easily be on familiar terms, if he wanted, Gregor never lets their prestige go to his head: he keeps his distance, always, being careful not to get too involved. Which doesn't take much effort on his part, given his cold and unsmiling nature. Only one couple finds favor in his eyes, and insofar as he is capable of such a thing, Gregor will become the intimate friend of the philanthropist Norman Axelrod and his wife, Ethel.

Since these are the days of the first motion pictures, which will give birth to that novel phenomenon, the movie star, we might as well use these luminaries to provide a quick portrait of the Axelrods. Tall, lean, wry but affable, Norman is a little like Lionel Barrymore, while Ethel, quiet and dreamy, has something of Pearl White in her eyes, and in her smile, more than a hint of the Gish sisters, Lillian and Dorothy. Whenever Gregor is with them, it's almost always in the presence of Mr. Axelrod's freshly hired assistant, the young Angus Napier, whose short stature and frightened face call to mind Elisha Cook Jr., whose career will take off only much later. Angus Napier works for Norman as a secretary, personal assistant, and chauffeur, and while he carries out his employer's every wish and command, he keeps his eyes on Ethel, too, as if eager to do the same for her.

Promptly invited to dinner chez the Axelrods, Gregor is soon dining there regularly once a week and then twice, on Tuesdays and Fridays. Tuesdays are private occasions, just three or four at the table, depending on whether Angus Napier joins them, but Fridays are for social gatherings of a choice and changing selection of Gregor's admirers, who are of quite diverse styles and professions, recruited, as we said, from artistic, scientific, and political spheres. The inventor has also become a cult figure among quite a few mystics and visionaries, and as occultists take an interest, increasingly weird characters begin dancing attendance on Gregor, hailing him as their beloved Venusian, a visitor to Earth from a distant planet who arrived in a spaceship or, in other versions, on the wings of a large white dove.

All this amuses Gregor, and given his long-standing

affection for birds and for the order of granivores in particular, perhaps he doesn't mind these stories that much, although he naturally never makes any comment. In the scientific community, however, such things do not go down well. Learned societies are gritting their teeth. Topsy-turvy, the reverse of the medal, the classic counterpoint to success: now some people start calling Gregor a crook, an imposter. And they're all the more eager and swift to call him a charlatan because he enjoys becoming a public personage, loves to shine, strut, blow his own horn in the newspapers, a sin his scientific colleagues find crass and unforgivable.

Still, his showmanship wins over crowds flabbergasted by his performances and his variety of props, among which are the many curious tubes, now his trademark, which he'll never get around to patenting or commercializing. He's wrong, too bad, he ought to—because that's another dirty trick coming his way: it will be fifty years before they're rediscovered as the first avatar of modern fluorescent bulbs, what will come to be called, with no small success, neon lights.

As for Westinghouse, absorbed in the battles between alternating and continuous current, a battle he seems about to win, he continues to ignore Gregor's excesses. Westinghouse is caught up in the thrill of seeing his system selected to illuminate the Chicago World's Fair of 1893, which will run for five months to celebrate the four-hundredth anniversary of the day Christopher Columbus set foot in the New World.

This exposition, which will inspire enormous public excitement, is just the beginning: now that he has succeeded in convincing the authorities that electricity can be transported over long distances, which is definitely Edison's weak point, Westinghouse gets the nod to begin by electrifying the entire city of Buffalo. Once the contract has been signed to install the whole infrastructure as an alternating current power grid, the company immediately begins building completely new electric plants. And the first of these hydroelectric facilities, twenty-five miles from Buffalo, will be constructed where Gregor wanted it, dreamed of it, imagined it, or foresaw it in his youth: right at the Niagara Falls.

11

AT THE CHICAGO WORLD'S FAIR, Gregor presents a new program and is once again a star.

Mustache waxed and precisely trimmed, lips clamped in a thin line, black hair with a blue sheen and parted in the middle to frame an impressive forehead: perched stiffly on a high dais before a packed and gigantic crowd, Gregor stares sternly at the audience for a long time, waiting for them to quiet down into complete silence—although this is just a pose while he's busy counting every last spectator, even those in the jump seats on the aisles.

A tall wading bird in a swallow-tail coat, white tie, and patent-leather shoes with thick insulating cork-lined soles that put him, along with his top hat, at close to seven feet, Gregor stands out at first against the gloom of the stage, but spotlights gradually reveal around him a panoply of high-frequency equipment. A dim alcove contains Gregor's softly glowing coils, fluorescent lamps, and his eternal tubes, all gleaming off and on as if they were breathing. Here and there, flashes of light dart crackling from revolving gears. Small copper spheres or ovoids spin all by themselves atop velvet-draped tables, reversing direction at regular intervals.

Gregor lets this initial silence last quite a while before he begins, without a word, to demonstrate a series of electric marvels at an ever-faster pace. At his direction and at a distance, as if by magnetic control, sparks are soon exploding all around, their brilliance at times shooting through the air in every direction, launched by Gregor's long arms—tipped with his very long fingers and seemingly endless thumbs—at lamps that start glittering frenetically.

As mystified by these scientific matters as I am, the audience at this point is already goggle-eyed and openmouthed at such a spectacle. When Gregor begins, however, in a crashing din, to pass between his hands currents in excess of 200,000 volts, which vibrate a million times a second and appear as shimmering phosphorescent waves—and then turns *himself* into a long cascade of fire, the crowd screams for the rest of the act. After which, in the gradually falling silence, Gregor's motionless figure continues briefly to emit vibrations and haloes of light that fade slowly into the returning darkness, until the audience holds its breath in a theater as black and silent as the crypt.

Then, when the lights snap on, the spectators blink and look at one another without daring to applaud, until they notice that Gregor and his paraphernalia have vanished from a stage that seems like a lacquered, immaculate, and empty screen, a mirror reflecting simply their own amazement.

Then, shaking off its stupor, the crowd rises in disorder to stream toward the exits, the men pensively donning their hats, the women automatically adjusting their ribbons and laces. The cleaning staff and usherettes have not yet begun to pace through the rows of seats, sweeping the floor and searching for lost objects, dropped hairpins, forgotten fans, discarded programs. The entire audience is gone—except for Ethel Axelrod, still sitting in the front row apparently lost in thought, dressed without ostentation that day in a bell skirt and a blouse with gathered sleeves, her entire outfit in a dusky pink, even to the little military collar cinching her neck. As usual she wears no bracelet, necklace, or brooch, and no ring other than her wedding band. Only after some time does she decide to leave her seat, long after Gregor has disappeared into the wings with a heady sensation of power, looking for the first available sink where he can wash his hands.

Outside again, Ethel Axelrod does not go to the Women's Building, which her high-society female friends from New York have hurried to Chicago to see and where, from the first

dishwasher to the innovative zipper, they can admire everything that promises to make their lives easier. When she
catches sight of her husband and young Angus Napier over by
the Ferris wheel, she does not go there, either, making her way
instead to the illuminated fountains specially designed for
the exposition. Engrossed in conversation with his secretary,
Norman Axelrod does not notice the distant presence of his
wife, whom Napier, however, has spotted.

Let's spend a few moments on Angus Napier. He's a short
young man who seems sullen, both frightened and dangerous,
although at times there's a kind of lost innocence in his eyes,
as naïve and stubborn as an angel's, which competes with that
weaselly look of his and creates the impression of a rather
crazed child capable of torturing someone to death while
clasping his victim tearfully to his breast, vowing lifelong love
and devotion between two sessions with a red-hot poker—
thus plagiarizing ex ante facto the physique and persona of
the aforementioned Elisha Cook Jr., who will be born in San
Francisco in ten years on the 26th of December, like Richard
Widmark, before coming to grow up right here in Chicago
and going on to spread his wings in Hollywood as a supporting actor.

Cherishing, let's agree on that, a hopeless passion for Ethel,
Angus Napier has managed to make himself indispensable to
Norman, doing his best as his secretary and hoping to remain
not too far away from his wife, who in spite of her kindness

and progressive ideas thinks of Angus as little more than a servant. Young Napier, however, has astutely observed Ethel's discreetly definite interest in Gregor, for whom an absolute hatred now burns in the secretary's heart. Seeing Ethel move off toward the fountains, he says nothing.

12

MEANWHILE, DRYING HIS HANDS on a single-use towel he has just pulled from his valise, Gregor goes over in his mind other spectacular projects based on electricity.

One of these days, for example, he really must—it's an old plan—envelop himself in a cloak of cold fire that, as he conceives of it, would warm a naked man at the North Pole and from which he would emerge not only unharmed but improved: mind refreshed, organs rejuvenated, skin renewed. Another medical angle: he should work on the idea of high-voltage anesthesia in hospitals. It would be equally advisable to bury high-tension cables under schools to stimulate the poorest students, while in theaters, electrically charged dressing rooms would put actors in the proper frame of mind and end the problem of stage fright. He'll have to get busy on all that.

But these are mere details, paling in comparison with his

new, more grandiose idea: the installation of a terrestrial nocturnal light, illuminating the entire planet from a single source. On that score, he would simply send rather high-frequency fluxes into the stratosphere, where there's a partial vacuum and the gases are of the same nature as those in certain light bulbs Gregor has devised. Thus one would not only light cities without having to use the classic street lamps—so costly as well as inelegant—but also greatly improve the safety of traffic by land, air, and sea.

Ordinarily Gregor doesn't discuss these plans much, except with certain international experts who visit him. When such visitors ask how he intends to conduct these currents to such an altitude, he shrugs, says it's easy, and leaves it at that. Always the same problem with him: one never really knows whether all this is possible or mere wishful thinking, unless it's pure bluff. Since he never reveals his methods before he has actually tested them, it can be hard to decide if he truly wants to develop all these things or if he's just being a smart aleck. In the meantime, for lack of money, his ideas remain just that: ideas.

For the moment, having trimmed his nails quite short and, to remove all the particles caught beneath them, washed his hands once more, Gregor smoothes his hair in the mirror before dashing to the station to catch the Chicago–New York Express. He'll have plenty of time to think all this over on the train.

13

Soon, however, money won't be a serious problem anymore.

Seven years later, Gregor is now rich, or rather, virtually rich, his position and prestige at Western Union allowing him to live very comfortably on credit. Rich enough to have made his home at the Waldorf Astoria, the chicest hotel in New York—and incidentally, the world—where he retains a large bachelor suite on a yearly basis. Gregor often dines alone at a set time and without ever consulting the menu, for he chooses his dinner himself, then orders it by telephone precisely one hour before he goes down to the Palm Room—the chicest restaurant in the chicest hotel—where, seated in a corner with his back turned so people won't bother him, Gregor is never served by a headwaiter, having long ago insisted that only the chief maître d' should take care of him.

We are in November, and tonight he must dine earlier than usual, since Westinghouse has announced his visit to the Waldorf in the very early evening. This slight change of schedule is a little annoying to Gregor, who is a man of order and habit, but both gratitude and self-interest persuade him that it would be inappropriate to argue with the entrepreneur's decisions.

When Gregor arrives in the dining room, twenty-one spotless napkins wait piled in advance on his table. Why so many napkins for a single man, you ask? Well, because Gregor's morbid fear of microbes has become such that he himself must, before eating, carefully clean his cutlery, dishes, and glasses, even if the crystal stemware in the Palm Room sparkles as brightly as its silver. And why exactly twenty-one, you wonder? Well, as you've been told, because that's divisible by three so it's very good, almost as good as the address of Gregor's laboratory: 33 Third Avenue.

So piece by piece, he shines all this tableware, which certainly hadn't asked for it, then with a curt wave he signals the maître d' to begin serving. Yet when everything is ready, still he delays eating because first he must estimate methodically—but instantaneously, he's used to this—the precise volume of every dish, the contents of every glass, the amount on every fork and in every spoon. Calculations all the more necessary in that without them he wouldn't be very hungry—in fact that mathematical exercise is actually what allows him to take nourishment. Because aside from that and without that, Gregor doesn't care *that* much for eating.

But there's more to it than estimating such quantities. He must also count the number of forkfuls, just as he continues and even increases, by the way, his efforts to count everything, because in this department things have not calmed down. The number of steps between the hotel and the lab. The number of buildings, vehicles, men, women, pigeons—more than ever, the pigeons—encountered on his walk. The steps of every staircase, even those he uses daily, going up *and* coming down, just to check or, perhaps, simply to keep from falling on his face. The escalator, invented in 1859, has not yet become commonplace but if it were, Gregor would doubtless count its steps, too, a perfectly fruitless undertaking. Although he doesn't keep track of his breathing, it's certainly not an oversight, he was tempted, and he hasn't decided if he's upset or relieved at having given up that idea, it depends on his mood. Still, he gained some free time that way, since always counting everything, well, it keeps you pretty busy.

Strangely enough—and you've heard this before too—Gregor doesn't behave like that with money. He's rich, though, and as everyone knows, often the more you have, the more you count it up. He could surely be richer but doesn't seem to care too much about that, satisfied with his standard of living without seeming to want anything more. Time, on the other hand, is certainly something he's been keeping track of for nigh on fifty years. When he looks at his watch every thirty-three minutes, however, it isn't to check the time; he always knows the exact time, because he has perfect timekeeping the way others have perfect pitch. And the fact that he just consulted his watch, by the way, is because after dinner, in his suite this evening, he'll be meeting with George Westinghouse, whose note making this appointment intimated that serious matters need to be discussed.

It's getting late. Gregor leaves the table, crosses the lobby to the elevator he hates using but what can you do, New York is vertical. The operator touches his cap, announcing the twenty-first floor, and Gregor already has his key in his hand. It's not that big a suite, but it's in the Waldorf, after all, which is very, very nice. Let's skip the curtains, wallpaper, artworks on the walls, bibelots. The medium-sized drawing room is furnished with three armchairs, a roll-top desk, a small safe, and there's a rather large bedroom. Gregor has just time to neaten up a bit, even though everything in his place is always neat as a pin, and when two quick knocks sound at the door, he opens it right away.

Mr. Westinghouse seems a trifle embarrassed, apprehensive, ill at ease, even after Gregor has shown him to the best armchair, then offered a cigar, then would he like a drink of some kind: bottles of whiskey, bourbon, cognac, and brandy stand on a tray, especially—exclusively—for visitors. Seated, Westinghouse accepts both offers but, without lighting the one or sipping the other, as if to gain time, he first pays Gregor a few compliments, albeit in a dull monotone: My, you've got a pleasant little place here, glad to see you've settled in so well. He seems, though, to be having some trouble finding his words. Well, he finds them in the end but then has trouble getting them out, now hesitating after the first syllable, now rushing the others along, now taking his own sweet time to figure out what the next one will be in a performance punctuated throughout with extensive throat-clearing and some nervous sniffing. All right, let's get to it, here's the deal.

In the course of bringing certain files up to date, Westinghouse's bankers have come across the contract signed with Gregor more than fifteen years earlier and which, in the euphoria of quick commercial success, everyone had somewhat forgotten. This contract stipulates—now a dim recollection—that Gregor be paid a $2.50-per-horsepower royalty, a reasonable sum at the time. Except that everything has turned out infinitely better than they'd ever imagined back then: over the last five years, the unforeseen amount of horsepower sold has become astronomical, and the horrified bankers have just calculated the accumulated royalties as yet undisbursed to Gregor at more than twelve million dollars. If this sum is paid, which Gregor could require, he might become one of the richest men in the world but here's the thing: that would place an unbearable burden on Western Union. His bankers have therefore urgently advised George Westinghouse to ditch this contract but he is loath to do that, and obviously can't break it unilaterally. That isn't done. There are laws. There are judges, there are courts, and they pass sentences. Above all, there are penalties that might make the situation even worse.

So Westinghouse explains this situation to Gregor, who listens to him gravely, silently, until he is done. Then Gregor gets up and goes to the safe, a simple model without a combination lock or code or formula or anything, and besides it's always open. He gets out the contract and, with his back turned, glances rapidly through it before returning to face the entrepreneur. Mr. Westinghouse, he says, you were the only one who believed in me. You have supported me, you have helped me, you have stood by me as a friend. All I ask of you now is to put my alternating-current system in the hands of the world. As for the rest, we'll never mention it again.

With those words, Gregor solemnly tears up his contract. Proving that in the dirty tricks department, sometimes he plays them on himself. May I freshen your drink?

14

An agreement is therefore reached whereby Western Union will completely buy out Gregor's patent rights for $198,000. A ridiculous sum compared to what he should have received, but it's as if he didn't realize that. Disagreeable and sure of himself as he is, with a self-regard as great as his disregard for others, one would expect him to negotiate shrewdly for his due but no, he seems not to see the implications of his self-esteem for his daily life. Still, he must know what he's doing—and of course he does: he's the first to develop the use of electricity beyond its illuminating and thermal applications. He is the pioneer in what will one day be called the electric everything. As such he could reap more rewards from his discoveries, ask for at least a slight percentage. Some form of profit-sharing, if only a tiny royalty or just a little raise in salary, I mean, whatever. But no, he's happy as is.

If he's not chasing after money, maybe it's because he'd

rather not have to think about that. Or perhaps he's satisfied just to live at the Waldorf, and rather grandly (always on credit, given his prestige), and above all, he enjoys perfect liberty in his laboratory. Maybe it's also because he doesn't really have the time.

For throughout the next ten years, many ideas—very many indeed—will strike him in big batches, but his mania for constantly coming up with these ideas prevents him from stopping long enough to *work* on one of them. Too many opportunities tumble around in his mind for him to go too deeply into them in succession, developing their practical applications and profiting from their commercial value. It's not that he's unaware of their worth, on the contrary, but he's too busy to follow through on that. He just files the patent applications, alerts the press with great fanfare, as he so loves to do, then turns his attention elsewhere.

So perhaps it isn't that Gregor is inventing things, strictly speaking, but that in the discovery and intuition of those things, he is content to provide the ideas that will produce them. He's making a mistake, going much too quickly; he ought to spend five minutes on an idea to carry it through, explore the possibilities, especially since his ideas are all so promising, see for yourself. Radio. X-rays. Liquid oxygen. Remote control. Robots. The electron microscope. The particle accelerator. The Internet. And so on and so forth.

As we all know, everyone always thinks up the same thing

at the same time, or at least there's always at least one person who has the same idea you have. But there's always someone, as well, who with the same idea as everyone else proves more patient, more methodical, or luckier, craftier, less overextended than Gregor, and by focusing completely on the idea, this someone beats everyone else in the world in the race to realize its potential. And it's this person, the winner, who gives his name to the idea. He's the one who puts it on the market, makes it his business, and makes the money. Perhaps all this hangs, once in a while, simply on a name. Take the movies, for example. A slew of people invented the cinema at the same time, but among them were two brothers named Lumière: Light. Everything can depend on so little, can't it; the slightest thing can tip the balance, and with a name like that, it isn't surprising that the Lumière brothers carried off the prize.

That's how it will go with Gregor: others will discreetly make off with his ideas while he spends his life bubbling away with new ones. But it's not enough to keep things boiling, one must then decant, filter, dry, crush, mill, and analyze. Count, weigh, sort out. Gregor never has the time to cope with all that. The others, off in their corners, will take the time they need to carry out his ideas while he, dashing on, will have already pounced on something else. And his patent applications won't help, won't any more keep Roentgen from claiming the X-ray than they'll prevent Marconi later on from saying he invented radio.

It's also that Gregor's a little pushy, always trumpeting his discoveries, less concerned with securely staking his claim than with making the biggest possible splash. And without stinting on the hyperbole, going all out with shameless exaggeration. Take the robots. Hardly has he come up with the concept than there he is, spouting away for the photographers: quite soon he'll be showing them an automaton that, all on its own, will behave as if it were endowed with reason, without the impetus of any exterior commands. Well, Gregor isn't there yet. Although one of these days, who knows?

But he does have one major preoccupation, based on a coil for electromagnets, U.S. patent 512340, which ought to allow the cost-free production of important quantities of energy, since a small part of that energy would keep the device itself running. A huge idea. Like a car that could constantly refill its own gas tank, yet use only a gallon to go a hundred gallons' worth of distance. This would be the first milestone in his chief objective: a system that would at no expense provide free energy to everyone.

This is another window onto his weird conception of money. Because his attitude does not jibe with the logic of big industry, which is always governed by self-interest. And although the newspapers fall instantly in love with this idea, announcing that Gregor will electrify the entire planet, that he has just found the way to transmit a universal energy without costing anyone anything, one can imagine that at the top echelons of companies listed on the Stock Exchange, this news causes account books to slam open, faces to frown, and voices to firmly suggest that measures be taken, that meetings be held to take a closer look at this guy.

In the evenings, however, still buoyed by success, Gregor often welcomes celebrities as before to his laboratory, where they happily pose for the first photographs lighted by gaseous tube lights and still love to watch Gregor complacently showing off in a shower of trailing sparks from his high-frequency transformers, or brandishing one of his long tubes of glowing glass—only this time, his other hand isn't touching any wire at all. Mysterious progress.

One evening, leaving his office, he spots a wounded pigeon hiding behind a trash can on a corner of the sidewalk, having dragged itself that far as if to die there in peace. Coming closer, Gregor diagnoses a broken wing and leg, but the pigeon returns his gaze with a weary look, as if advising him not to bother, before turning its round eye away. As Gregor continues his examination, however, the bird, seemingly touched by his interest, returns his gaze, and for a long time, they contemplate each other as if they were about to speak.

Delicately, he picks up the creature, wraps it in one of his three spotless white handkerchiefs, then gently stows it beneath his jacket, near his armpit, as if covering it with a wing. Then, without a thought for the dreaded microbes that everyone knows infest the plumage of these filthy pigeons (not to mention fleas, ticks, lice, mites, and tiny flies), he takes it back to his room at the Waldorf.

Before turning his attention to first aid, and always happy to putter around, Gregor first builds a kind of nest out of cardboard and bed linen. Next, of course, he disinfects and nourishes the patient before splinting the injured limbs with tiny arrangements of pins and matchsticks secured by rubber bands.

Since Gregor is pretty knowledgeable about anatomy, too, the bird is quickly patched up and Gregor, anxious to respect the house rule forbidding animals in the rooms, builds a cage that he moves discreetly to the hotel's roof. After three days of convalescence, the pigeon flies free in tiptop shape. And Gregor is rather pleased.

15

ON THE TUESDAY MORNING IN QUESTION, Angus Napier has a full schedule.

He must attend a meeting of various heads of companies, then a "business" cocktail party, and lastly a social luncheon, all at three different locations in Manhattan, but luckily they're not too far from one another. He therefore dresses carefully that morning in an outfit suitable for each occasion, combining administrative decorum (three-piece suit and black tie) with the relaxed yet still formal atmosphere of a cocktail gathering (pocket square and colored tie), tweaked with a touch of worldly elegance (buttonhole flower and fantasy tie) for the luncheon. Such versatility isn't easy, but he pulls it off, intending to change ties twice while en route in a cabriolet between events and adding, during the last ride, the flower.

Edison Electric has merged with another firm, so it is now

the General Electric Company that has arranged the meeting of these company directors, which takes place at GE headquarters. The guests are heads of various businesses exploiting energy sources (petroleum, coal, wood, natural gas), modes of transport (by ship and rail), real estate (construction and estate management), and communication. Thomas Edison himself is there, of course, for he has invited all the others. As Angus has foreseen, discussion focuses almost entirely on Gregor's recent pronouncements, at the mention of which brows furrow even more fiercely and voices rise to an even higher pitch, because this business of *free energy* has sparked lively differences of opinion. Although some still consider Gregor a flamboyant charlatan and claim that his recent so-called discovery can't stand up to scrutiny, others argue that his unexpected triumph in the upper echelons of Western Union makes him a real threat: he has proved his inventiveness, obtained real results, and this insane, dangerous idea of cheaper energy might just well succeed. During the general excitement, Angus Napier elbows his way through the throng to the side of Thomas Edison, who doesn't give him a single glance.

After Angus manages at last to catch the great man's attention, there are a few false starts, given the inventor's deafness and the need to avoid being overheard by others, so Angus finds talking to him an undertaking even more complicated than getting properly dressed that morning. Once he has

Edison's ear, however, Angus persuades his host to follow him over to a quieter corner of the conference hall. After they converse briefly, Edison says a few words, inaudible in the surrounding hubbub but which seem to indicate acquiescence. Evasive acquiescence, nuanced by a gesture of withdrawal, the kind one makes to shed responsibility, show one has washed one's hands of the matter, before promptly walking away. Those words and that gesture appear to satisfy Angus, however, and after a bow, seeing no more reason to linger, he quietly leaves the meeting to hail a cabriolet outside.

At the business cocktail reception over at Westinghouse, the atmosphere is entirely different. There almost no one is talking about Gregor and his speeches, except to eventually sing his praises for having so impressively plumped up the firm's profits, and in any case they let him talk away about whatever he wants. Instead the guests rejoice at the increasing growth of their vast electrical networks, the construction of ever bigger production units, the successful development of new steam turbine techniques, and a possible future monopoly on the propulsion of freighters, steamers, ocean liners, and other large vessels. As the guests offer toast after toast, Angus slips away.

It's time for the luncheon, one of a sort frequently held in private dining rooms in hotels or in palatial restaurants to fête Gregor, who is often surrounded by a rotating cast of celebrities—today, for example, Mark Twain—but always closely protected by his intimate friends, an inner guard here reduced to the Axelrods, toward whom Angus makes a beeline. About fifteen people are chatting among themselves, although turned above all toward Gregor, the cynosure of all eyes, for in him the art of pleasing is full of contradictions: as brilliant and lively, even excitable, as he is quiet and reserved, even curt, or melancholy and mysterious, even abstruse— Gregor knows how to seduce everyone but lives alone, and attracts the most diverse individuals, men and women alike.

And as it happens, a number of women are present, some married but others on their own and who, finding Gregor to their taste, cast velvety looks his way, discreetly but availably, while the wives' glances are in the same key, with a little less vibrato, of course. Alas for the ladies: among other quirks of character, Gregor seems little inclined toward physical contact, which he avoids less from a fear of germs than from an absolute horror of hair, which is as frightening to him as naked electric wires are to everyone else. And he still detests jewelry, finds its jingling irritating, its sparkle garish, its cost alarming. Particularly fearsome are earrings, because that hook through the flesh is chilling, and as for pearls—their milky appearance and bivalvian provenance repulse him to the core. Unaware of all this, however, and competing with one another to bejewel themselves seductively, the ladies thus lose a little more ground each time before retiring empty-handed, hiding their dismay with complicitous but hopeless looks and silvery laughter grown tarnished and dull.

Only Ethel Axelrod, in fact, appeals to Gregor. Soberly elegant (a devoted reader of *Harper's Bazaar*), she wears almost no makeup and never any jewelry except—too bad—her wedding ring, which complicates everything, since Gregor could never do a thing to hurt his kind friend Norman. Perhaps in other circumstances he might allow himself to go after someone else's wife but this one, no, not this one. And although Gregor himself embodies—and senses that he does—the ideal man in Ethel's eyes, she finds it impossible to envisage, given this particular husband, etc.

This husband has just been chatting with Mark Twain about the events of that year, waxing indignant mainly over the war with Spain. Mark Twain champions rallying, like William James, to an anti-imperialist league, whereas Norman makes gentle fun of the American army's lack of proper sanitary equipment, given that fewer than four hundred soldiers were killed in combat while more than five thousand died of yellow fever, dysentery, and food poisoning. Trying to insinuate himself into this conversation, Angus is of course aiming to get within striking distance of the Axelrods so he can approach Ethel, but in vain, since she remains stubbornly turned toward Gregor like the mesmerized needle of a compass.

Ignored, diminished, struggling to master his bitterness and humiliation, Angus leaves the table before the meal is over, under a pretext that meets with indifference. Hailing another cab, he returns resolutely to the offices of General Electric to pursue his work as an informer, whereas Gregor, after the dessert, coffee, and liqueurs from which he has as always abstained, returns—obstinately alone—to his lab.

16

BACK IN HIS LABORATORY that Tuesday afternoon, feeling somewhat melancholy, Gregor sits down in a chair instead of getting right to work. This social whirl—how tiring it is to be always inside oneself, with no way out, constantly considering the world from within that imprisoning envelope. And unable to show that world anything of oneself save an exterior painted on somehow or other thanks to mirrors. Not much desire for anything, all of a sudden. Little bout of sadness.

Well, inactivity isn't like him, not Gregor, who knows nothing of boredom, usually too busy with his train of thought, chugging along full time in spite of everything, almost without his say-so. Looking idly around the lab, he begins studying the massive iron pillar that supports the entire building vertically from floor to floor like a spinal column. After a while, he has an idea and rummages through a toolbox until he finds what he's seeking for his experiment: a small electromechanical oscillator of his own making, no bigger than a deck of cards.

Having strapped the oscillator to the side of the pillar and turned it on, Gregor sits down again, curious to see what will happen. And gradually, affected by the vibrations of this seemingly benign device, small objects here and there in the lab establish resonance with the oscillator, one by one. Gregor sees them shiver, then tremble; hears them murmur, then hum. The resonance quickly spreads to bigger things: the furniture and even other equipment begin jumping more and more briskly, shimmying badly enough to start warping. Soon everything is dancing. Thoroughly engrossed in this phenomenon, Gregor in his chair has forgotten all about his fit of the blues.

Unbeknownst to him, however, this very low-frequency vibration has gradually affected the pillar itself, which seems—imperceptibly at first—on the verge of becoming sinusoidal. So there's nothing to prevent this vibration from affecting the basement—now shaking in turn—before coursing on to the substructures of Manhattan one after another as if via an earthquake, which as everyone knows increases in intensity as it radiates out from its epicenter. Gently at first, but with increasing severity, the surrounding buildings thus begin to shake, crack, split, as their windows explode singly to begin with—then en masse.

Within a few minutes the frantic tenants of these buildings

scramble pell-mell downstairs and out into the street, most of them to stare petrified at the swaying facades while others run to alert the authorities. Let's quickly point out the presence in this crowd of young Angus Napier, who appears promptly at the scene, his usual frightened expression betraying nothing beyond the ordinary. It's not long before he's joined by two men, apparently acquaintances: one seems to be disguised as a thug, the other as a layabout, which in fact accurately represents their respective social status as gangster and unemployed lout.

At the local police station, it's determined that this unusual earthquake is not affecting any other section of the city—and is in fact limited to the area around the building containing Gregor's paraphernalia. Since the inventor has already acquired a solid reputation as the fabled "mad scientist," suspicion immediately falls on him, so two officers are dispatched to see if he is indeed up to something.

Given that his building has not been shaking as much as the neighboring ones, Gregor had not at first noticed the extent of the phenomenon, but now he is alarmed to feel the vast rumbling coming from the floor and walls of his lab, where everything is quivering, with even the pictures on the walls coming alive in their frames like little movies, until the very air itself now seems to groan, a painful sensation that leads him to end the experiment.

When the policemen burst into his laboratory, Gregor

has just demolished the oscillator with a sledgehammer. He brusquely shows the officers to the door and waits for his inevitable moment, which isn't long in coming: for the reporters and photographers who hurry there as he'd expected, he improvises—as always in such circumstances—a press conference during which he announces, in his arrogant and megalomaniacal style, that he has discovered a way to destroy in a matter of minutes—if he so chooses—the Brooklyn Bridge or the New York World Building, take your pick, or even both at once if you like. Well, such a performance won't help his reputation but Gregor, you'll have figured out by now, is not trying to keep a low profile, not by a long shot. And one fine evening shortly after this event, his laboratory goes up in flames.

It's only reasonable to feel that Gregor's experiments have grown too dangerous to be conducted in a big city full of unsuspecting, naïve people. Not to mention that his coils produce tensions up to several million volts and shoot enormous dazzling arcs, lightning bolts several yards long. It's not inconceivable that such excesses are growing increasingly risky, and that someday an accident is bound to happen. One might tell oneself that. One might also wonder about the presence that evening among the onlookers, filing his nails as he watches the blaze, of the unemployed man, along with the gangster, who were with Angus that other day. However it started, the fire spares nothing: destroying the machines, melting the equipment, reducing files and archives to ashes, it consumes in a few hours what Gregor will mourn as the work of half a lifetime.

Another dirty trick played on Gregor who, uncertain but never discouraged, consults his lawyer, who thinks that instead of pursuing rash legal remedies the inventor should find another place to work, more isolated, farther away. Since the lawyer happens to be a shareholder in an electric company over 1,600 miles west of New York City, he suggests that Gregor move out to Colorado Springs, where his company will provide him with free electricity. Well now, says Gregor. A change of air, why not? Let's go.

17

As a matter of fact, the exceptionally dry, clear air in the mountains of Colorado crackles with static electricity. There Gregor will find a suitable atmosphere for his projects, more numerous than ever, which he is eager to get up and running again. In addition to his experiments on atmospheric and terrestrial electromagnetic waves, he intends to perfect a worldwide system of wireless telegraphy and, above all, work on his idée fixe: discovering the means of transmitting energy absolutely free and unfettered to the far corners of the planet. So the first thing to do, naturally, is build a transmitter.

Out in Colorado Springs, Gregor stays at the Alta Vista Hotel. Since he distrusts elevators, Gregor and his belongings go up only one floor, where he chooses room 207, which is no better than any other, but its number has the advantage of being divisible by you know what. He instructs the chambermaid to supply him daily with eighteen fresh towels, and informs her that he would rather do his own housekeeping. That taken care of, he and his assistants set off in a buckboard wagon for the site reserved for him.

The sun shines brightly in Colorado, where there are also frequent violent storms, one of which even produced up to six thousand lightning bolts in one hour. It's the ideal research location, the perfect playing field for Gregor, who claims to have hyperacoustic hearing—unless he's a mythomaniac, that's always the problem with him—and to hear lightning over six hundred miles away when his assistants strain to detect it at around one hundred. In any case, the mountainous site suits his desire for secrecy and mystery, surrounded as it is with pastureland roamed by indifferent horses, while the closest building is an institution for deaf-mutes. Having inspected the panorama, various animals, and local birds, Gregor pulls from his briefcase a sheaf of plans that he unfolds on some wooden sawhorses. Now he's ready to contact the local building tradesmen.

He soon has his transmitter, a square wooden building crammed with coils and transformers, capped with a kind of turret from which projects a tall metallic mast, itself topped with a copper ball. With this mast, connected to a powerful high-tension and high-frequency oscillator, Gregor undertakes to simulate storms, modest ones at first, which gradually become spectacular. Such experiments soon grow quite noisy but, as he's out in the middle of nowhere, they probably won't bother anyone. Besides, they always take place at night when Colorado Springs is asleep with the lights out, so electrical usage is at its lowest ebb and Gregor can allow himself to make ample use of the local power company.

On those nights, when he's ready to turn on his apparatus, he and his assistants are careful to protect themselves beforehand with cork-soled shoes, insulating gloves of felt or asbestos, and cotton plugs that just about reach their eardrums. Then, once the release has been tripped, vivid bolts of lightning leap up one after another, denser and longer lasting than those in a real storm and bristling with scintillating aigrettes, those quivering brush discharges of residual electricity, until all the lightning rods within almost twenty miles around are linked in a circle beneath the tumult of electric arcs.

All this makes a mighty uproar but doesn't really disturb the neighborhood until one night when Gregor, in his enthusiasm, goes too far and creates a hellish din. Suddenly, all Colorado Springs is startled wide awake by this crashing racket, and terrified locals rush in their nightshirts—on horseback, by buckboard, even on foot despite the distance—to see what's going on. Dumbfounded but keeping a respectful distance, convinced this artificial lightning can annihilate them with one strike, they are at first petrified with amazement and then jolted into life by the webbing of incandescent particles flitting among the grains of sandy soil and burning with intense light even beneath their heels. People begin dancing clumsily, the way we've all seen cowboys do in Westerns when someone shoots at their feet, while around the laboratory, long sparks spurt hissing from every metal object touching the ground, and out in those pastures, the placid horses pick up shocks through their shoes, rearing and bolting with foam-flecked mouths, whinnying more wildly than at any premonition of the slaughterhouse or knacker's yard.

This much-talked-about adventure is the subject of a lengthy chronicle in the town paper, over which the good citizens wax indignant at first, then relax into mere displeasure, and end by feeling somewhat indulgent and not a little proud at the idea that such an eminent and puissant scientist has elected to live in their backyard. Colorado Springs calms down, until the night when Gregor blows it by trying to emit an electromagnetic wave that this time will grow stronger and stronger—why not go all out?—until it establishes resonance with the earth itself.

The necessary currents will be higher than ever this time, for the voltage must reach into the millions. Gregor has dressed solemnly for the occasion: a gleaming bowler, pale pigskin gloves (brand-new), and a Prince Albert coat. He completes the reverse countdown and holds his breath; then, when his assistant turns on the switch, an enormous flash explodes above the laboratory, which fills with an icy blue glow and the strong smell of ozone while giant bolts shaped like skyscrapers rocket from the mast with crashes more thunderous than ever. This marvel continues for a few minutes, increasing in intensity, until abruptly everything stops: no more light, no more noise, and above all—no more current, not even enough for a tiny nightlight.

Furious, Gregor sends one of his assistants to the Colorado Springs Electric Company. The man finds the town completely plunged into darkness and learns from the terrified night watchman what is then confirmed by the captain of the firemen: the powerhouse's main generator, overloaded by Gregor's experiment, has exploded and caught fire. Summoned the next morning, Gregor is curtly informed by the company director that his service is being cut off—and will be restored only when the generator has been repaired at his expense, a repair promptly effected within a week by Gregor's men.

Colorado Springs is once again glowering at Gregor: the local press did not enjoy the power outage, some people snub him in the street, and the number and cleanliness of the towels delivered daily to his room are not longer quite up to his standards. Undaunted, he pursues his research, often sleeping on site and only for a few hours at a time because he's pushing himself relentlessly, until he finally completes his system for wireless telegraphy, for which he hastily files the patent applications—but too hastily, as it happens, and probably rather carelessly.

On another night when he's working with his powerful

radio receiver, Gregor thinks he hears strange noises that seem to come from extremely far away yet are melodic and display a regular rhythm. Thirty years later they will be recognized as radio waves that indeed come from the stars, but Gregor, always quick to get carried away, doesn't hesitate to solemnly attribute them to distant sentient beings native to other planets—Venus or Mars, at the very least—who are gifted with intelligence or even scientifically more advanced than we are and are trying to communicate with him. That's something else again.

Still as fond as ever of attracting attention and creating a bit of mystery, Gregor promptly lets it be known that he's in touch with Martians. This announcement is sent joyfully throughout the country by the newspapers, which just adore this, having long recognized Gregor as a goose that keeps laying golden eggs, and they wouldn't miss a chance to make fun of him for all the tea in China. The scientific community, however, dignified and staid, is less appreciative of this kind of stunt. Pleased with the new publicity, and all the more tired of living in the country now that he's becoming so unpopular there, Gregor decides to return to New York. He feverishly packs his bags, now preoccupied by this nagging question: What should he reply to the Martians, and *how*?

18

AND REALLY, COLORADO—enough of that. Fresh air is all very nice for a while, but it's time to go home. And let's get going because the money's all gone, so we must find fresh funds to finance new projects.

It isn't the burden of isolation that sends Gregor back to the big city. He never misses the company of men, since he's content to be alone with his machines, or the company of women either, since he's just as content alone in his bed, where he doesn't spend much time anyway. What he needs, in fact, is the company of rich people. The diners at the Players, Delmonico's, and other establishments frequented by useful possessors of capital. From whom Gregor, through brilliant and subtle sweet talk, has always tried and often with success to extract the necessary backing for his research. Although he does need to go home for this purpose, it's equally true that in the comfort department, returning to the Waldorf

Astoria—where a line of credit is always open to him—will be a welcome change from eight months at the Alta Vista Hotel.

So for close to a year—the last one of the nineteenth century, as it happens—Gregor has been able to play with lightning to his heart's content up in the mountains, discovering stationary waves, using the earth as a lab instrument, and receiving news from extraterrestrials. That's not a bad scorecard, but—it's time for something else. The something else is the construction of a gigantic tower, and this time it will be a station for his wireless "world system" of communication. Now *that*, Gregor feels, should appeal. And above all, attract capital.

They're ready for him in New York, however. The scientific community still hasn't gotten over that business with the Martians, which so discredited Gregor in their eyes that they roll them heavenward in disgust at the very mention of his name. As for the newspapers, delighted to seize afresh upon this perfect caricature of a crackpot, they never let up, saddling him with a reputation so grotesque that passersby grin when they see him, the Waldorf's elevator operators turn away with a snicker when he steps into the cabin, and even the children of these scientists, journalists, passersby, and elevator operators follow him down the street shouting things at him. But Gregor doesn't give a hoot: the construction of the new tower is now his chief preoccupation, followed by the need to pay for it somehow. Well, he knows that in spite of everything, at least the financiers to whom he will appeal for funds still take him seriously.

These men cannot forget, it's true, that in spite of his now laughable reputation and all his colleagues' efforts to discredit him, it was Gregor who, through his alternating current system, assured Westinghouse the American monopoly on electricity; in other words: an inexhaustible gold mine. So it's certainly conceivable that an idea of similar caliber, coming from the same individual, might be nicely able to provide them with a likewise hefty fortune. They know he is eccentric, of course, and given to sudden enthusiasms, but the stakes are worth it, so they must simply remain alert, keeping a close eye on him while leaving him free to think. Keeping the other eye out for possible profit, they can afford to ignore his sinking reputation, and one after another of these men listens attentively to Gregor when he pitches his new project, spinning it in a way that can't help but interest them.

Now he's talking about a worldwide system of information made possible by broadcasting over several full-spectrum channels, carrying radio programs, private communication networks, stock market bulletins, and telephone interconnections, among other possibilities. Provided that it can become a reality, this idea for a wireless transmission monopoly seems like a high-paying proposition at first glance, and the rank-and-file bankers show immediate interest. They want to know more, invite him to dinner, and introduce him to the managing directors of various companies. Seeing this eagerness on the part of the money men, Gregor decides to aim higher and tries to contact the most powerful among them: John Pierpont Morgan.

It isn't easy to approach J.P. Morgan, since his importance allows and even obliges him to protect himself from the world. Well, look how things work out: one of the few people who see Morgan socially outside banking circles is also one of Gregor's few friends: Norman Axelrod. Gregor has looked up Norman since returning to New York, but prefers to meet him alone and in public places rather than at his friend's home, because he fears seeing Ethel again, with whom he has an emotional bond all the more troubling in that it's mutual.

Yet the day comes when he must have lunch with them. He and Ethel behave with strict propriety, punctuated now and then with discreet glances. The conversation moves tolerably along until coffee is served, after downing which Norman excuses himself, he says, to fetch his cigars in the living room. There follows a long silence. So, Ethel remarks at last, you spent quite a while in Colorado. Well, replies Gregor, a year. That's to say, a short year. And you didn't write to me once, she points out to him. Forgive me, but I was so busy, mumbles Gregor, not even trying to hide his bad faith. But, you see, I didn't write a thing to anyone. Besides, he ventures, you know perfectly well that I'm a bad sort. But me, too, says Ethel with a smile. I'm a bad sort, too.

Such a reply opens up so many possible perspectives that Gregor's eyes open wide indeed. Women do not talk like that in 1900. Ethel does. New silence, during which, after staring at her too long, Gregor seems fascinated by the bottom of his coffee cup. Ethel keeps smiling even when Norman returns to the dining room with his cigar box in one hand and in the other, a letter of recommendation to John Pierpont Morgan.

19

OF ALL THE FINANCIERS Gregor will ever get to meet, John Pierpont Morgan is the richest. In fact he is the most power-ful one in the world, for his interests—and the dividends they earn—encompass the most varied and traditionally profitable domains: petroleum, gas, coal, timber, railroads, shipping, real estate, and those are just the highlights. A Jupiter of the dollar, a Frankenstein in business, J.P. Morgan is a callous and short-tempered brute whose tripartite motto is: Think a lot, say very little, write nothing down.

Unusually burly, with the shoulders of a pachyderm and the glare of a python, J.P. Morgan prefers to keep as much as possible out of the public eye—and keep his picture, in any case, from circulating at all. If he hates nothing more than being photographed, however, it's less from a desire for privacy than on account of his nose. No man has ever been or ever will be saddled with such a nose, and no one will suffer so much from such an enormous purple appendage creased with crevasses, pimpled with nodules, webbed with fissures, prolonged with lobules, and bristling with hairs. In the rare photographs of him we have, even though instructions were always to retouch them upon pain of death, Morgan always seems about to have the photographer executed.

He is the monster—known nevertheless for his success with women—whom Gregor undertakes to entice with the prospect of this monopoly: the control of all future radio stations throughout the world. This prize missing from Morgan's trophy case, which instinct tells him could earn a fortune, is the perfect lure to charm the financier. Especially since Gregor can be eloquent at will.

Eloquent but discreet. For he is careful not to reveal the true—and for him, essential—purpose of his communication station. Aside from its accessory function as a means to chat with Martians (a subject on which he has finally learned, since it occasions ridicule, not to expound), the main goal of this station is to realize Gregor's first whimsical idea: to produce and supply to the entire world energy that is always available, to everyone, gratis. Through means known only to himself and which must remain so, his future generator will function without any outside source, without any further need for mankind to toil at gutting the earth for fossil fuels. Done with all that: thanks to his new system, the power of the future will be free.

But Gregor is better off keeping this major aspect of his project to himself. Mum's the word, especially since the idea of the communication station is enough in itself to obtain the desired funds: $150,000 flutter in an instant from Morgan's coffers toward Gregor's bank account. Light-headed with joy, the inventor slathers the financier with fawning blandishments, modestly remarking that neither Christopher Columbus nor Leonardo da Vinci could ever have succeeded without noble patrons like him. The noble patron calmly points out, as he hands over the contract, that he has reserved for himself 51 percent of Gregor's radio patent rights as security for this loan—a word on which he lays some emphasis.

Once the contract is signed and locked away, J.P. Morgan, charmed by this fresh promise of profits, suggests that they celebrate and takes Gregor for a drink to a vast tavern called Tannenbaum's Oyster, on the corner of the avenue where he has his offices. For despite his aversion to appearing in public, the great man does not disdain to mix occasionally with the populace.

Tannenbaum's Oyster is full of people, smoke, noise, shouting, player-piano music, and the clatter of glasses at this busy hour, but everything stops at the arrival of the financier, instantly recognizable, for he is preceded by his legendary, luminous, and voluminous nose, which is like a vehicle with an emergency light at the head of a convoy. In the respectful silence that immediately falls, John Pierpont Morgan steps with weighty tread to the bar to order, growling like an ogre, two beers that the bartender swiftly provides, trembling slightly. Then, considering the customers frozen in a circle around him, each respectfully clutching his hat with both hands to his chest, the financier decides to create a touch of ambience. When Morgan drinks, he roars, everyone drinks.

Ovation. Enchanted by this prospect, the customers all order at least one beer straightaway, and conversations resume with the clink of beer-mug toasts. The music and joviality roll merrily along again until John Pierpont Morgan, having speedily drained his glass, slams a dime down on the bar with an impact that imposes complete silence once more. Everyone turns again toward Morgan, who surveys the room before hollering once more. When Morgan pays, he booms, everyone pays. Followed by Gregor, he moves briskly to the door, the dismayed customers rummage through their pockets, and the construction of Gregor's tower can begin.

20

THIS TOWER: here's what the inventor has in mind.

Supported by a cubical structure and capped by an enormous electrode, it will be constructed of wood, 187 feet high, octagonal, in the shape of a truncated cone, and will enclose a thick steel shaft sunk deeply into the earth and encircled by a spiral staircase. The main building, of brick, will contain instrument, boiler, and generator rooms, as well as a laboratory connected to a living area with modern comforts. As for the electrode, a globelike dome forged from copper, Gregor had first seen it as doughnut-shaped before switching to a mushroom cap. The whole thing would thus have a fungiform aspect, a bit like a gigantic cep.

That being the design for the tower, the question becomes where to put it. In the end, a site is found on Long Island, at the shore, not too expensive or hard to reach, 62 miles from

Brooklyn, an hour and a half by train. That choice made, it's time to get going, and they do.

While they do, as workmen get busy by the dozens, Gregor doesn't waste a moment. Ubiquitous, he appears everywhere at once as if he'd been multiplied by four: at the work site, offices, laboratory, and social events. Constantly checking on the station's progress, hour by hour and down to the last detail, he also spends all his days in his new facilities on Third Avenue, conferring with other scientists from all around the world, and he hasn't forgotten to work full time as well on many new research projects independent of his tower. For example, after coming up with a new kind of radio-controlled torpedo—always useful in a war like the recent one with Spain—he devotes his spare time to discovering and developing various things, simultaneously writes a few dozen articles, and himself types up, doubtless with some extra hands, the patent applications for his new finds as well as their practical applications. As for what's left of his days and nights, Gregor spends that at glittering receptions at the Waldorf or Delmonico's, where he's still the toast of the town.

And whenever does he sleep? That, no one knows; perhaps he doesn't sleep at all. And whenever does he fuck? There's nothing to show he does that, either, it being not inconceivable that he hasn't quite enough time to be more than four people all at once. Ever present, ever lively and efficient, it's only with regard to his patent applications, perhaps, that one might blame him for proceeding too hastily at the risk of proving negligent.

No one would dare blame him for anything anyway, not even or certainly not Ethel, in spite of the intimate although tacit and elliptical complicity that binds her to Gregor, who still dines faithfully with the Axelrods every Tuesday and Friday. Without realizing or admitting it to herself, Ethel is much too solicitous of Gregor's feelings, of his sexuality (if he even has any), too entranced by his person to allow herself to intervene in any way in his professional life. Much too busy doing her hair, choosing a dress, and perfuming herself on those Tuesday and Friday evenings, and then when he arrives, being too careful not to stare endlessly at Gregor as he holds forth on how the construction is going on Long Island, while Norman sees debonairly to the cocktails and young Angus Napier, who sometimes attends these dinners, furnishes his frightened face with a tight smile and keeps his feelings carefully in check.

Well, as this tower intended to launch the very first radio transmissions is rising into the air, now we learn from the press—on the front page of the *Philadelphia Inquirer*—about a spectacular but unfortunate event. A certain Marconi, Guglielmo by name and a native of Bologna, has just kicked the props out from under Gregor's entire project. A young man with a long thin nose and a melancholy smile, far from New

York and armed with his patent 7777, this Marconi shamelessly announces his invention of radio.

He has indeed managed to send a wireless telegraphic message for the first time across the Atlantic, from Cornwall to Newfoundland, demonstrating that radioelectric waves can cross long distances following the curvature of the earth. The message itself is simply the three dots of the letter S in Morse code, but the harm is done. Marconi is really first, and will reap the merit of this invention. Universal astonishment, for the most part; Gregor in particular at a loss.

There is immediate amazement that Marconi has achieved his ends through such simple means. People wonder about him. They are unaware that he merely used one of the patents—645576—filed by Gregor a few years earlier but without sufficient protection. They have no means of knowing that this patent was mailed anonymously to Marconi. Were anyone to learn this, one might consider, studying the handwritten address on the envelope, if it displayed any features in common with the penmanship of Angus Napier. Even though priority of Gregor's work in radio transmission will be recognized by the United States Supreme Court forty-two years later, in the meantime, forty-two years earlier, it's another dirty trick played on him.

The ink is still wet on the *Philadelphia Inquirer* when he's urgently summoned by John Pierpont Morgan. Well, says the financier, so it's not worth anything anymore, your gizmo, right? You saw that Italian fellow, hmm? He didn't need that enormous contraption to transmit. One moment, replies Gregor, let me explain the whole thing to you.

His hand has been forced: he plays his last card, lays everything out. Revealing that radio transmission was only one of the incidental uses of his monumental tower, he finally unveils its main purpose: his free power plan. Until now he had felt it wiser to keep quiet on this point, knowing that it involved a conception of money incompatible with that of the market; investors finance in principle only what generates profits, and anything else makes them grind their teeth. But, well, the great John Pierpont Morgan might be touched by the vastness of the enterprise, you never know.

But really, of *course* you know: Morgan won't be the least little bit touched. Having never embraced the profession of philanthropist, the financier shows no enthusiasm at the idea of delivering current as free as the air to countries peopled by penniless Moldavians, Ainus, or Senegalese. Assuring Gregor that he continues to enjoy his deep personal sympathy and moral support, Morgan cuts off all credit with a stroke of the pen. Work on the tower comes to a halt at the snap of his fingers. Screwed again.

Please understand me, Morgan points out. It doesn't work at all, your system. If everyone can draw on the power all they like, what happens to me? Where do I put the meter?

21

ALONG WITH ALL THAT, which goes swiftly by as his life always does, Gregor is closing in on his fifty-fifth year. When days seem so long and afternoons drag on forever, one never realizes how fast one can wind up middle-aged without knowing quite how that happened, even if, like Gregor, one consults a watch all the time—although this gives only an imperfect, biased, and, frankly, false idea of that notion.

What with his constant activity, but especially after these latest reverses and failures—the blows he knows, believes, or doesn't realize have been struck at him—perhaps he might worry about himself, reconsider his methods, and modify his relationship with the world. He'd have good reason to do so, even though he seems not to understand this. Arrogant, sure of himself, Gregor hasn't changed his ways at all, still going out every night, following more than ever the men's fashions of his day, and keeping his suite at the Waldorf, where from the maître d' to the bellhops, he dispenses tips as extravagant as his own opinion of himself. He buys big advertisements in newspapers to justify himself on point after point, claiming to have made every new discovery, promoting the merest hint of an idea before subjecting it to the slightest experimental verification, heaping scorn on his rivals and contemporaries in general, in short—becoming increasingly unpleasant.

Well, all this is costly, whereas he is now broke, in debt, living hugely beyond his means and only thanks to credit. Unwilling to drop him altogether, Morgan does slip Gregor a little something now and then, never enough to cover all his expenses, alas, but above all, for some people never change, only as a loan. Trying to rake in more funds, Gregor again uses his laboratory occasionally for those spectacular shows he does so well, before audiences of what he can still find in the way of nabobs, hoping to lure money from their deep pockets. Warily, though: only the very wealthy need apply, being too ignorant to steal his ideas. Not a single scientist is invited anymore, out of caution.

Other than that, daily at noon on the dot he arrives at his company headquarters. After his two female secretaries greet him at the door to take his hat, gloves, and walking stick, he enters his office, where the blinds have been lowered and the curtains carefully drawn, since Gregor cannot concentrate except in perfect darkness. Daylight may only enter during storms, when, lounging alone on his black mohair sofa,

Gregor watches the sky and the lightning crackling over New York. As it happens, he is becoming not only more unlikable and increasingly embittered, but perhaps a little unbalanced as well: some suspicious signs are appearing. He has always talked to himself, keeping up a running monologue while he works, but his worried secretaries can now hear him—even through the padded door—ranting more than ever during these thunderstorms. At such times, he seems to be addressing the lightning bolts themselves as if they were employees, children, students, or his peers, and he employs an astonishing variety of intonations: consoling, stern, plaintive, affectionate or threatening, humble or grandiloquent, or mocking, with delusions of grandeur.

Worse, when these tempests have passed and no matter what the weather, Gregor is beginning to talk outlandishly at any time, frequently about ideas so grandiose that his friends, or what's left of them, attempt to protect him against his own declarations.

Megalomaniac though he may be, he now invents a new turbine. A turbine, you'll say, is always just a turbine, but it must be admitted that this time the turbine is exceptional. Indisputably lighter and more powerful than the rest, it seems destined to put its inventor back on top and in the spotlight. Gregor, faithful to his sense of nuance, modestly announces that he sees no limit to the uses of his bladeless turbine, which will henceforward power all automobiles, trucks, trains, planes, and even ocean liners, speeding them easily across the Atlantic in three days. Operating indifferently on steam or gasoline, less expensive to make than traditional turbine engines, this invention will prove equally irreplaceable in domains as diverse as agriculture, irrigation, mining, hydraulic transmissions, and refrigeration. Exclamations, applause, glory, and fresh hope: Gregor is over the clouds when he sees the first applications of his turbine, which initially performs superbly but soon shows its limitations.

A telling indication, perhaps, that Gregor's scientific genius is at an end: having miscalculated his estimates, he has to agree that the turbine is a lot more expensive to make than anticipated. Another thing he hadn't thought of: the advantage of its high rotation speed proves to be a defect, for although this speed is indeed incomparable to that of earlier engines, it is so extreme that no metal can long withstand the stress. Result: end of the turbine.

End of John Pierpont Morgan as well, who dies in the meantime. After remaining up to then, even reluctantly, Gregor's chief cash cow, he leaves the direction of his affairs to his son, who will soon be importuned in turn.

End of the year, in any case. On the occasion of these festivities, Gregor sends suitable greetings to John Pierpont Morgan Jr., hoping his holidays will be happy. Still, times are hard, he points out at the end of his letter, and I confess that I am desperate. I need money terribly and can find none anywhere. You are the only one who can help me and, as I beg for your assistance, I wish you a Merry Christmas.

Then he consoles himself by going to feed the pigeons of Reservoir Park, which no longer even bears that name: rebaptized Bryant Park, it's near where the great public library will soon rise. Gregor goes to that park every day now. Reducing his social life more and more, he seems to have transferred it to these wretched birds, for which he has lost none of his affection.

He enters the park, and even before he takes from his pockets the bags of seed he's brought for their Christmas presents, the abject birds recognize and pounce upon him, cooing horribly by the dozens as they cover him entirely, pecking frenetically and convulsively into pockets that are coming undone. Enveloped head to toe in this blanket of small creatures, barely breathing so as not to disturb them, Gregor stands motionless near the park gate, through which passersby, who have stopped with their large beribboned packages in the lengthening shadows, stand staring at him and shaking their heads.

THESE FESTIVE SEASONS, Gregor knows them well. Protect himself though he may, swathing himself in clothing and goodwill, the cold finds its way through to him the way weariness attacks his neurons. Even though he has thought of everything beforehand this time, being used to the experience and thus determined to weather it with equanimity, the same thing always happens and overwhelms him: he is helpless and the situation, hopeless.

Gregor loses all interest in things during this period, hasn't even the slightest firm opinion to rely on. If there's no snow, that's too bad, he misses it, and besides, at least it would look pretty. But if snowflakes then grant his wish by falling, that's immediately really too bad because they soon turn to mud. Same thing for presents. If he's given a present, it's a crummy one. If he gets none, let's not go into that. Or into the dinners people break their backs to organize, either, taking such pains with the menu—because the more the food looks lovely and smells good, the more it all tastes to him like cardboard.

It's in this bitter frame of mind that he leaves his hotel and heads chez the Axelrods, who have invited him—and there's no way out—to their damned party. Tonight the streets are crowded with carriages tinkling with jingle bells, lined with bands mistreating hymns that were dreary to begin with, carolers warbling ridiculous songs on the corners of avenues decked with ugly polychrome garlands, and uniformed Salvation Army stalwarts as well as Santa Clauses in all formats ringing bells, while the sidewalks overflow with an excited crowd, their hats pulled down to their purple ears, wrapped presents tucked under their arms. Gregor must nervously thread his way among men already drunk, women scolding frantic kids, plus landaus, pushcarts, and wheelchairs.

Welcomed by Ethel's lipstick-red smile and the matching Bloody Mary held out to him by Norman, Gregor first rubs his hands before the fireplace the way one does in those situations before offering one's gift. He has brought a glass star of his own design that sparkles mysteriously all on its own, with constantly changing radiance and color. Standing on a chair while the Axelrods applaud, Gregor attaches the star to the top of the tree already decorated with traditional ball ornaments, ceramic angels, and tiny candlesticks. Then everyone sits down to a classic festive dinner—let's skip the time-honored menu—during which, at the dessert, the

Axelrods give Gregor their gifts: from Norman a calfskin-bound edition of Wordsworth, and from Ethel a moiré crêpe-de-Chine tie.

Even though he already has plenty of ties and zero interest in Wordsworth, Gregor hides his bad mood at the party. The fact that he's not smiling is not unusual, and when necessary, he can seem sociable until the moment arrives, determined by delicate temporal calculations, to take his leave as soon as possible after lingering just long enough for no one to imagine that he's bored stiff. The single incident that warms his heart a little: as she walks him to the door while Norman, his back turned, pours another round of his revolting digestifs, Ethel—perhaps a tad tipsy—knots his new tie playfully around his neck. Despite his aversion, even with her, to physical contact, and despite his sudden irrepressible fear for one second that she will strangle him, he finds to his surprise that he enjoys this moment. A little erection, Gregor? Go on, just this once.

Back at the Waldorf, wearing his tie and carrying his Wordsworth, Gregor finds in his mail J.P. Morgan Jr.'s reply to his letter. This reply is a bill for $684.17 in interest accrued on his father's loans to Gregor, along with the heir's best wishes for the season. So there's nothing more to hope for in that direction; the coming year is looking dicey indeed.

Waiting for better days, Gregor will live through many that are almost empty, unusually sterile for a man who has never been idle. Going to bed earlier, getting up later, he goes less often to the office, and when he is there, he hardly leaves his black sofa. In his spare time, feeling at a loss—all his time seems lost to him, actually—he plays around with rather uneven ideas regarding the propulsion of fluids and comes up with various projects almost immediately abandoned: an automobile tachometer, a tidal wave generator to swamp dreadnoughts, and an aircraft without wings. This last consists of a parallelepiped—a three-dimensional figure formed by six parallelograms—shaped like a kitchen gas stove, supposedly capable of flying in and out of a window if need be. This idea might make us smile, if we were in the mood, because at first glance it seems like something that will never get off the ground. And yet we'd be wrong to smile. Fifteen years later, this idea would meet with great success as a vertical takeoff and landing aircraft, but too late for Gregor, in spite of the patent application he ritually files.

Anyway, Gregor no longer seems to believe much in all this. His modest glory and social success notwithstanding, his string of failures leaves him for the first time with no desire to do anything. Without bitterness or resentment, he has nothing more to do but wait and see, that's it, since life is now only a long waiting room without even any rumpled magazines lying on a table or furtive glances exchanged with other patients.

23

His creditors are waiting around, too. Since Gregor has always tended to forget them as if they didn't exist, they've been biding their time for so long that they're not too sure about that anymore either. As if, even under a cloud, a personality of such worldwide renown completely overshadowed their paltry private selves, preventing them from coming forward to claim their due.

Through a reverse effect, considering himself grandly above all laws, Gregor has perhaps come to think of them as having actually wound up in *his* debt, their letters of credit becoming in his eyes letters of nobility, conferring such honor upon them that Gregor is repaying them handsomely with his debts: in that light, it would even be petty, not to mention dishonest, for his creditors to demand repayment. These debts, however, keep accumulating and growing larger, and the creditors keep thinking about them. Thinking about them more and more seriously. Until the tiniest pressure would be enough to tip the whole situation in the other direction.

It will be a minor business over local taxes, a modest sum and one doubtless considered by Gregor beneath his dignity, that provides the fateful pressure: caught in the workings of bureaucracy, he finds himself in court like any other peon. And since the tax department—which is not an actual person—has stepped in, the law seems to provide the idea, the example, and the authority to individuals to make their own moves. Now everything comes swiftly together, and accelerates, yet nothing works out: it appears that Gregor is even more penniless than anyone, even Gregor, had thought, since his bookkeeper never got up the gumption to bring this to his attention. Gregor must admit that not only has he been cleaned out, he also owes enormous amounts of money to enormous numbers of people including many tailors, shoemakers, custom shirtmakers, restaurateurs, florists, and other tradesmen, not to mention subcontractors, and especially the folks at the Waldorf Astoria, where he has been living in luxury, on credit, for years.

I'm aware that Gregor is so unsociable and unpleasant that one might think he has simply gotten what he deserves, but still. Here he is flat broke and threatened with prison just when Edison, Westinghouse, Marconi, and all the rest are profiting from his ideas acquired at bargain prices (when they weren't stolen outright), flying high in business, and raking in money. Wiped out, Gregor realizes bitterly as well that numerous enterprises based on his own inventions, from alternating current to wireless telegraphy and including X-rays, are flourishing without even waving a dollar in his direction. It's unfair, but Gregor, with his well-known talent for conjuring up glittering miracles, will manage to save himself by making the rounds of multimillionaires. With $100,000 here, $150,000 there, he collects enough to pay off most of his debts, and, to settle the rest, he sells the land on Long Island where his tower sits unfinished. He must also reconsider his faltering lifestyle and leave the Waldorf for the St. Regis Hotel, where he moves in on the fourteenth floor, which isn't divisible by three since he no longer has the clout to impose his caprices, but his new digs aren't all that bad either.

The tower on Long Island, however, is finished enough to look suspicious to the U.S. Army, which considers it a possible base for espionage and demolishes it six months later, because the United States has just gone to war and not to just any war, not like that little rumpus with Spain twenty years earlier. This is an all-out world war, impressively deadly, and—since the age of aerial bombing has not quite arrived yet—it's being waged in particular at sea: sinking 35,000 tons of Allied shipping daily, German submarines are becoming a real problem.

Reading in the news that the Naval High Command is frantically looking for a way to detect these submersibles,

Gregor—always on the qui vive—remembers one of his old ideas. A murky business involving stationary waves, pulsating energy, intercepted rays, and fluorescence, it seems like a perfect solution to the problem, and Gregor hurries to submit it to the general staff. Who, rolling their eyes in unison when he walks in, smilingly send him on his way with a promise to be in touch, but once he's gone, they dismiss the latest lunacy from this crackpot, wanting nothing to do with it. The authorities will wait for another world war to roll around before they find Gregor's idea not so silly after all, since it will become a universal means of defense known quite simply as radar.

By the way, says Gregor when he returns to the charge the next morning, if you're interested, I have a few other ideas. The shoulders of the dismayed general staff droop at his arrival, then shrug at his proposals. This is something really fine, he explains: a flying device without crew, wings, or engines and that can be remotely launched to go drop bombs anywhere in the world, as far away as you want. Not bad, hey? Noses turn up as one at the description of this bizarre and improbable object without a future—although it will later become quite familiar to us as what we now call a guided missile. We'll think about it, his audience tells him, and keep you posted.

Right, says Gregor: I also have a robot ship, if you like, isn't that interesting? But no one is even listening anymore, they're all looking off into the distance, rubbing their heads and lighting cigars, waiting for him to get tired and finally go away.

He is unpleasant, he has many faults, but he's no fool. Realizing that no one is listening to him and that no one ever will, Gregor seems to give up on the idea of offering others the creations of his mind. He even appears to lose his effervescence. His secretaries watch him slowly change his daily routine, as if he were resigning himself to idleness, and soon they too will be idle, for he will no longer be able to pay them. Less often at the office and in his lab, Gregor frequently goes in particular to stroll around Grand Central Station, even though he has no train to catch. More regularly, in fact every day now, he visits Bryant Park to feed his eternal charges, and when he can't go, he enlists the friendly services of a Western Union messenger who has earned his trust, a young man with a special hobby: raising homing pigeons.

24

THE PIGEON: I mean, really.

The skulking, deceitful, dirty, boring, silly, feeble, mindless, vile, vain pigeon.

Never affecting, deeply unemotional: the pathetic pigeon and its stupid voice. Its rasping flight. Its dull stare. Its ridiculous pecking. The annoying back-and-forth jerking of its brainless brainpan. Its shameful indecision, its tiresome sexuality. Its parasitic vocation, absence of ambition, blatant uselessness.

Inferior to the stylish magpie, the voluble blackbird, the crow—which is not without class—and the sparrow with its modicum of charm; worse than the vulture, which at least has a purpose in life; as appealing as a rat, as aristocratic as a horsefly, less elegant than an earthworm, and even dumber than the mythical catoblepas, said to have a hog's head on a buffalo's body.

One would kill a pigeon as casually as if it were a cock-roach, but it's so insignificant, why bother? Forget kicking it—too much trouble, or too embarrassing—except for a bit of exercise, and even then the bird's not worth it and might soil your shoe. And don't argue that the carrier pigeon has been of service now and then in wartime, lucky at that to have found itself a piddling job as a flying object.

Nasty pigeon, not even good to eat, disgusting on its bed of mealy peas. And yet it really is what's becoming Gregor's favorite and soon only dish, as the inventor winds up dining exclusively, alone in his little room, on the bird's white meat, sliced from the breastbone. Strange.

Yes, that does seem curious but one can try to understand. By imagining that through some special logic, given that Gregor feeds the pigeons, it isn't inconceivable that they might nourish him in return. One might well also reflect that loving them as he does, he must love them completely. One should above all remember that when buying at the butcher's, pigeon is not very expensive.

25

Because now Gregor really is stone broke. Although the management of the St. Regis is willing to overlook his unpaid bills because he has moved to a single cramped room, he can no longer frequent the hotel restaurant. He can no longer maintain a laboratory or local office anymore, either. And since Gregor still tries to keep busy, even if it's only for appearances, he has had to exchange his bookkeeper for the hired hands at an accounting service and his secretaries for the young, pigeon-fancying Western Union messenger, who isn't too greedy for tips and works as his part-time errand boy.

The Axelrods having set him up in an office in a tiny little room in the Blackstone Hotel, there Gregor will try to sell a few projects for new machines by mail order, but these inventions seem increasingly conceived just for something to do, less from conviction than through the sheer automatic habit of inventing. An elastic-fluid turbine. An improved lightning rod. A locomotive headlight. A hydraulic turbo-alternator. All advertised, in Gregor's characteristically humble style, as innovative if not revolutionary, easy to operate, high-performing, and—simply put—of overwhelmingly superior quality.

Well, these ventures, like so many others, will never come to anything. And not only because of the indifference of his contemporaries, as Gregor mournfully maintains. Because in a man's life, it sometimes happens as well that nothing works anymore, that the inventory of fixtures falls into disrepair. Here and there, bit by little bit, one sees how the mind deteriorates: just like matter does. It happens via addition and subtraction: sly elements join in—dirt, dust, mold—while precious ones degenerate through wear, fatigue, erosion. And then there's the corrosion that attacks, chews up, and devours nerve cells the way it does atoms, producing all sorts of slowdowns, cracking joints, aches, negligence, and hit-and-miss messiness. It's a long, tortuous process, imperceptible at first, but which can sometimes, abruptly, become as plain as day.

As when Gregor has an idea that no one, as far as he knows, has ever had before. It's a bold process, the degasification of copper, thanks to which the metal, now free of gas bubbles, will be denser and therefore much improved. Gregor finally manages to pitch this intrepid conception to a metallurgical research facility. Impressed by his reputation, the engineers consider his proposal but quickly figure out that champion electrician though he may be, Gregor knows little about the science of metals. Having given him an appointment and knowing him to be touchy, they treat him with careful consideration, using the softest of kid gloves to explain that his audacious system—although most interesting—cannot possibly succeed: it is all the more difficult to extract gas bubbles from copper because copper, you see, has no gas bubbles to extract. So it really isn't strange, they tell him gently, that no one ever thought of his system until now. Gregor silently gathers up his papers and withdraws, smoothing his mustache.

It also happens that he files a series of patent applications he hasn't even properly thought out yet, for some hasty work on fluid mechanics; the patents are recorded not without indulgence, and even a touch of pity. It happens more and more that when Gregor offers his services as a consultant to all and sundry, the projects, evaluations, reports, and prospectuses he has drawn up are systematically turned down, and the few companies he stubbornly sets up quickly prove to be duds. All this, on average, produces nothing but crumbs, simply serving to repay a few outstanding debts and provide the errand boy's salary about half the time. Well, even though the young man doesn't ask for much, there's a limit, and Gregor's errand boy begins combing the want ads.

If Gregor begins to withdraw even further from society, it's not just that he can't afford to go out, because now even his desire to see people is fading. He's never been much of a drinker, but ever since the beginning of Prohibition, he has disliked its consequences: the atmosphere has changed, and he finds what will be called the Roaring Twenties—wood alcohol in speakeasies, flappers, the Charleston, Al Capone, Al Jolson, gilded youth, and market crashes—somewhat shocking. As the company of men, not to mention that of women, begins to grate on him, all he basically has left are the pigeons.

And there Gregor moves up a notch, exchanging his role as their nanny for that of their nurse: now he won't simply feed them, he'll take care of them. Having boned up on pigeons and doves, he soon prides himself on his expertise regarding their habits and customs and above all, their anatomical pathology. Equipped with a first-aid kit, he tirelessly roams the streets, docks, parks, studying these birds and spotting alarming signs in their behavior—depression, weight loss, a wheezing cough, any limping or arthritis, diarrhea, torticollis—so that he can attend to them immediately. Plaster casts, injections, disinfection, massage: he applies the therapeutic remedy appropriate to each case, although he will not intervene when the symptoms are too serious, when a pigeon begins to walk backwards, for example, or can't see well enough to peck up grain. Gregor knows that such behavior is due not to the proverbial foolishness of the species, which he denies outright, but to the paramyxovirus, which is always fatal and resolved only by euthanasia, which Gregor refuses to perform.

The thought naturally occurs to Gregor, while he's at it,

to move from outpatient treatment to institutional care by setting up a pigeon clinic. Which raises the question of premises. Since the management of the St. Regis would be most reluctant to house this endeavor, Gregor knows he cannot shelter too many long-term patients in his room. He therefore decides to take in only one at a time, on a case-by-case basis, for short-term or emergency care. To this end, he rents a large aviary from a fowler near the hotel for use as a waiting room, where he can keep his patients before their consultation. Meanwhile, he pursues his theoretical and practical studies—perfecting his skills in the care of crumpled wings, broken legs, gangrene and alopecias, quick to diagnose fowlpox at a glance, identify gout, detect nematodes, distinguish emphysema from aerophagia—and consults a veterinarian only about the rarest disorders.

His passion does not stop there: increasingly unwilling to be separated from his patients, Gregor resolves to flout the hotel rules by keeping a small group in his room, which he readies beforehand with homemade nests of wire, string, and cotton. Then late one night, after distracting the attention of the night concierge through some subterfuge, he smuggles a large covered crate containing six ailing birds up to his room on the fourteenth floor.

At first he limits the patients to a small rotating group, no more than half a dozen. Since he must sometimes be away tending to what's left of his affairs at his Blackstone office,

Gregor entrusts his charges to a chambermaid, who for a small sum will keep his secret and follow strict instructions regarding the birds. Soon Gregor will expand his operation, however, and the nests will multiply, for there is no lack of invalids: fifteen wounded pigeons will be in residence, then twenty, thirty, and the chambermaid will not be able to handle them all, so Gregor will have to hire two other hotel maids to take turns sitting at their bedsides. The patients will start cooing fortissimo, the fourteenth floor will begin to smell funny, other guests then lodge complaints—and the management of the St. Regis will summon Gregor to demand that he shut down his avian clinic.

This done and the premises disinfected, Gregor must first resign himself to his solitude, limiting his caretaking to daily visits to the aviary, now a dispensary where he regularly brings new patients and works toward their recovery. But things aren't the same anymore; he always leaves there feeling a bit sad and sometimes, to avoid returning to his empty hotel room, he tries to lift his mood with another walk around Grand Central Station, or else—this afternoon, for example—he goes to get a haircut.

26

FRESHLY COIFFED, CLOSE-SHAVEN, mustache recalibrated in a slender trapezoid, Gregor emerges an hour later from his barber's little shop, next to a ladies' hairdressing establishment where, the fashion for long hair having passed, a woman is sweeping out onto the sidewalk great hanks of hair swirled in a fluid mass with interlocking zones of blond, brunette, red, and black tresses, plus the occasional swatch of white or gray. That is where Gregor spies, limping in the blond section where it has come to grief, a new pigeon.

Gregor studies the bird. A long platinum blond or Titian red hair has wound itself among the toes of its right leg, and since the left one is now tangled in it too, the creature is hamstrung. With each move the pigeon makes, the hair digs deeper between the scales on its legs, an ever-tightening ligature that is cutting off the circulation. Thus paralyzed, the bird tries in vain to fly away, unable to lift off simply by flapping its wings, a twin-engine aircraft without a proper runway.

When Gregor tries to rescue them with the very kindest intentions, some pigeons prove absurdly recalcitrant, struggling like an old lady being helped across the street without her permission, even wounding him with their beaks and claws, but he has no trouble capturing this one. Securing its beak with a rubber band to keep it quiet, concealing it under his overcoat, he brings it discreetly back to the St. Regis, against the hotel rules.

Up in his room, Gregor first gives the pigeon a footbath of warm water and disinfectant. Leaving the patient to soak, he prepares the proper operating equipment: scalpel, tweezers, toothpick. Three hours later, judging the tissues sufficiently softened, he tries to discover in which direction to unwind the offending hair. Then, slipping the toothpick between the leg and the embedded bond, he cuts the hair into segments with tiny strokes of the scalpel, removing them with the tweezers.

Twenty minutes later, Gregor is done and estimates that two or three days of rest will have the bird back on its feet. Meanwhile, though, he contemplates it. He contemplates it at length. He contemplates it so much, hour after hour and almost in spite of himself, that an emotion of a hitherto unknown kind and format seems to steal over him as he watches. It's an attentive ravishment, a marveling; it's pleasing and rejuvenating, a steady, pure current that he has never experienced until now with anyone, and at the end of the day he finds himself wondering if it might not be an emotion he has only heard about and never paid attention to before, a feeling difficult to define, hard to put into words. A state—let's take the plunge: let's call it love.

This pigeon is in fact a female with feathers of the truest white, wings delicately striped with pale gray, her breast faintly tinted with mauve. Her scarlet beak is dotted with saffron yellow, her legs shade from royal purple to pearly gray and, immaculate, her tail tilts up just a little, like that of a peacock. Her genealogy must be exotic, moreover, because her eyes, usually round in granivorous birds, are not only slightly slanted but even—uniquely—edged with lashes. The soft, throaty timbre of her voice, her elegant, hesitant gait, and her way of tilting her head to one side, glancing away as if in nostalgic reverie, strike Gregor to the heart and seem almost to bring tears to his eyes.

A sign of weakness in him, perhaps; the reviviscence of his former ideas of grandeur, or the beginnings of senility. His rational mind cannot help it: this pigeon reminds him of how some excitable souls used to claim, back in the days of his young glory, that he had arrived among us on the back of a dove. Then Gregor's still fertile brain imagines that something like a conversation might arise between him and her, which isn't any more inconceivable, after all, than a chat with Martians.

So he takes care of her devotedly in his room for an entire week, after which, cured of her motor handicap, she ought to be released in accordance with the hotel rules. First off, however, although she has recovered perfectly from that leg business, the pigeon still seems a touch under the weather, droopy and tired. One could of course decide that such symptoms simply reflect a normal convalescence, which the bird should spend at the aviary. But secondly, Gregor must admit that he couldn't bear that. He has grown so attached to her that he would suffer to see her go. Unbeknownst to anyone, in defiance of hotel regulations, he decides to have her live in his room, as if she were the fiancée he has never had.

This secret bond cannot be maintained in a state of constant togetherness, however, since what remains of Gregor's business affairs still requires him to leave his room from time to time, and everyone knows that living together involves telephoning the beloved at least three times a day when separation is unavoidable. Thus Gregor must rely once again, in the utmost secrecy and thanks to exorbitant tips (considering his budget), on the housekeeper of the fourteenth floor to take care of the bird in his absence. When he is delayed by his projects or obligations, she must answer his six daily phone calls to report on the condition of the pigeon, which she also feeds according to a carefully arranged diet, a selection of fresh and varied seeds that are permanently stockpiled in the hotel room.

Among Gregor's obligations, the sole survivors of his society days are the ritual dinners on Tuesday and Friday with the Axelrods. Since his hosts notice after a few days how strange and preoccupied he seems, the inventor must account— through veiled allusions—for the appearance of someone new in his life, but, aware of the eccentricity of the situation, Gregor doesn't dare admit that he's talking about a bird. Misunderstanding, Ethel initially displays a feigned interest, followed by masked irritation and then straight jealousy concealed by coldness. Since a lover cannot remain silent for long, however, or keep from discussing his passion in detail at the first opportunity, Gregor must explain that the object of said passion is not what one might call a mistress but a minor member of the family Columbidae, which at first provokes amusement and sharp relief in Ethel.

But since Gregor, once the news is out, can't help sharing more and more news, and quickly starts talking about the pigeon as if it were a human companion and not a pet anymore, and soon talks about nothing else, Ethel's amused relief gives way to aggravation, then exasperation, until the jealousy is back and sharper this time because it's tinged with incomprehension and resentment—if not contempt—and camouflaged with even greater coldness, all to the complete satisfaction of Angus Napier.

The young man with the frightened face, meanwhile, has made himself a more solid place at Norman's side but no longer in his shadow. Now an individual in his own right, he is more than just a secretary, something halfway between an associate and an adopted son, consolidating his place with the Axelrods without giving up on one day seducing Ethel at last, although he is losing faith in that prospect.

Two other small developments have changed things for Angus. The emoluments he receives from Norman have permitted him, by dint of savings, first to acquire on credit and secondhand a lovely streamlined Duesenberg convertible with a straight eight-cylinder engine, a sleek torpedo with green flanks and a blue top, its large brown fenders protecting spotless tires with bright yellow rims and spokes. No car is more chic or more costly, and Angus has gone heavily into debt for this one, which is too big for him. Although you could never see this in his eyes, more frightened than ever by the expense, Angus is very pleased with it. As soon as he can, hoping to take Ethel on her errands, he puts the Duesenberg at her disposal. She turns down his offers most of the time, however, and now that Prohibition is a thing of the recent past, the second small development is that Angus tries to drown his sorrows over this impasse by drinking, it must be said, immoderately. Thus the glare he turns on Gregor is still as hostile as ever but pretty glazed and, given his perpetually frightened expression, not all that noticeable either.

As for the looks Gregor gives his pigeon, they're increasingly worried. Her health still seems precarious, so he attempts to get her back in shape by varying her diet or taking her for walks along the Hudson and on the beaches of Long Island, to build up her strength with sea air, or, trying out his old theories, with light electric shocks he administers with an ancient dynamo. One fine morning, he even sends her on a vacation, entrusting her to his errand boy—whose parents live in the country—with an absolutely endless list of dos and don'ts. Naturally he hates to part with her, but he'll try anything to restore her health, which a week of fresh air can only improve. Gregor finds himself dreadfully alone by the end of that morning and spends a long dreary afternoon holed up in his room without managing to work—an increasingly frequent problem—or even read the papers, which he leafs through distractedly. He's preparing to dine alone in his room a little earlier than usual when a clattering noise at the window makes him turn and she's there, pecking weakly at the glass, exhausted from flying home on her own. And Gregor's heart, when he lets her in, is pounding.

In the days that follow, nothing seems to go well, though. Indifferent at times to her food, the bird displays an extreme lassitude and there are moments when she seems dazed, moments soon marked by light coughing that grows hoarser, spasmodic, alarming, and coupled with fevers. In spite of his skill, Gregor must urgently summon a veterinarian. After long auscultations and palpations, a retinal exam, a blood pressure reading, and three taps of the reflex hammer, the doctor looks up at Gregor with doom in his eye. By way of a diagnosis, he slowly shakes his head. Like Madame de Beaumont, author of *Beauty and the Beast*, and the Lady of the Camellias, the Goncourt brothers' heroine Germinie Lacerteux, Fantine, Claudia, Francine alias Mimi, and other classic heroines, alas—there is no doubt: the pigeon displays all the symptoms of tuberculosis, and that illness, in those days, was still a sentence of death.

27

TEN YEARS LATER, before he gropes around under the bed for his shoes, Gregor puts on his socks. Slowly he slips them on with that serious look men his age sometimes have during such activities, the solemn expression of an elderly only child: careful, conscientious, cut off from the world and concentrating on the task at hand.

True, his body and the décor have changed. The hotel space has again shrunk around him, leaving only an attic room overlooking a courtyard, and while his manias have grown inexorably stronger with age, his gestures are weaker and a trifle more disorganized, often with a light tremor. When he glances out the window, he can no longer contemplate the vastness of New York as he could still do from his fourteenth floor at the St. Regis, with a view of the entire city all the way to the river. Gone, the great sky alive with lightning above the horizon. Outside the windows of the New Yorker Hotel, where he now resides, there is only a blank wall in front of him, and behind him, mounted on a stand, the white pigeon, stuffed.

After she died, he'd had her buried with great ceremony. Then, almost immediately, he'd had her dug up and her remains taken to a taxidermist. But even stuffed, according to the exasperated management of the St. Regis, she continued to attract parasites, a pure pretext, for the most worrying nuisances were the unpaid bills that finally led to Gregor's eviction.

So he had to move, year after year, from hotel to hotel, all of them within the same area but each time reflecting a drop in prestige that matched his failing fortunes. Going first to the Pennsylvania, he then fell back on the Governor Clinton, at last coming here to the New Yorker, which is much less gleaming and much less popular but much less expensive and where, most importantly, the management is willing to ignore the birds he has with him, by the dozens.

At seventy, alone as always in his room, he has almost finished getting dressed this morning. His clothes are still properly clean and pressed, but they no longer come from the same tailors as before, although Gregor has kept some garments from happier times, carefully preserved to be worn only on great occasions, which are growing rare. Of his two hundred shirts, for example, he has only a half dozen left, and the rest of his personal effects have been reduced proportionately.

Some of his shirts, worn at the cuffs, are also a bit shabby at the collar, so Gregor has had to learn how to sew a button back on, mend a hem, and a dressmaker on the corner will turn a collar when it wears through. Gregor has noticed, as it happens, a strange odor from the shirt he just put on, a faint, acid, dusty smell with a hint of rancid butter. The shirt has seen better days, true, but he puts on a fresh one every morning, and Gregor sighs, resigning himself to the thought that this phenomenon must come from his own body, from its weariness and wear.

So, he carefully puts on his socks. They are long, knee-length socks that require a certain technique: after he has pulled up a pant leg, Gregor centers the end of the sock on his toes, lining it up with his ankle so that the heel will be in the right place. Then he slowly draws the sock up his calf without making any wrinkles. Putting on his shoes, he methodically ties the laces in a bow, the loops of which he ties again. It isn't very stylish to double-tie laces and Gregor never used to, but it's safer. This way the laces won't come undone during the day, obliging Gregor to bend down to retie them, and such movements, he's been discovering more and more lately, exhaust him.

Although Gregor's eyebrows are still black, his hair is now thin and gray, and though he doesn't feel vain enough to dye his brows to match, he did finally shave off his mustache, which had remained black as well. He's almost as slender as before, however, alert and agile, although a little less lithe, but his figure is doubtless the result of a rather strict diet. For although it's true that the restaurant in the New Yorker is not as fine as those of his previous hotels, that question no longer arises since Gregor cannot dine there. Unable to afford even a normal diet anymore, he lives on warm milk and crackers, always the same brand, which he obtains in enameled tins that he keeps when they're empty. After the hotel management gives him permission to have a carpenter install shelves along a wall of his room, Gregor puts what's left of his possessions in those tins, now carefully numbered. The opposite wall is taken up by his pensioners, housed in cages constructed by the same carpenter, who has even built to Gregor's specifications a tiny stall with curtains, where each pigeon showers three times a week.

During the first months after his move to the New Yorker, Ethel comes to see him occasionally but soon, too proud to allow her to closely follow his decline, Gregor refuses to let her visit him. He sees her only outside, specifically in the public squares where she accompanies him and buys him packets of birdseed while their conversation flags.

But only on the subject of love—which has never explicitly come up, in fact—because Gregor is still a fount of information about his projects, and he returns endlessly to his old dream of universal energy, about which no one wants to think anymore. He constantly assures her—and everyone else he can buttonhole, although their numbers are dwindling—that he has worked out a completely original idea for tapping energy that is available night and day and year round, to be produced and delivered by an apparatus as simple as one, two, three. Ethel is an old lady now and lets him talk away; everyone lets him talk away, just as they indulgently let him publish in a few minor journals—after a discreet intervention by Norman, it's almost like self-publishing—his plans for two more projects: a geothermal steam plant and a system to generate electricity from seawater.

Gregor knows, however, that these rather dated ideas simply rework old themes, so it would be good to find something new. And he does. The specter of world war looms once again on the horizon, and this time Gregor comes up with a real corker: a powerful, invisible, incredibly destructive particle beam, proudly baptized "the Death Ray." The ultimate weapon.

Based on the principle of particle acceleration (when particles travel so fast that a small number can convey tremendous power), this weapon could stop a racing car, a speeding boat, or a plane in flight by simply melting them. Such a defensive apparatus would render any nation, large or small, weak or strong, indestructible by enemy attack from land, sea, or air, and its dissuasive strength would eventually make even the possibility of war unthinkable. The ultimate weapon indeed, and the harbinger of world peace. Forty-five years earlier, that had already been the idea, for what it's worth, behind Alfred Nobel's explosives.

When the *New York Times* charitably reports on Gregor's latest invention, its readers find the news sensational, but the entire scientific community just shrugs it off as usual, while only Hollywood starts dreaming of the wondrous possibilities of this disintegrating ray—if one doesn't skimp on the special effects. In short, everyone still lets him talk away, all the more easily in this case because after his grand announcement, Gregor hasn't much to say. Tightlipped about the full scope of this project, showing some discretion for once, he's being doubly cautious. First off, he fears that, as has often happened in his life and in the course of science, the same idea might be germinating in other brains as well and that he'll wind up being robbed again—he has coped with that too many times; he's almost used to it, but enough's enough. Most of all, though, he's afraid that the exploitation of his idea might benefit only one country, even his own, which would sabotage his objective of world peace.

Deciding to make his idea inaccessible to any single nation, one night he spreads his diagrams and notes out on his table and armed with scissors and a pot of glue, he cuts his plans into six interdependent sections, so that each one contains some information but is useless on its own and, like a puzzle piece, becomes truly meaningful only in light of the other five parts. Gregor spends the entire night on this. At dawn, he's done. He puts each section in an envelope, waits for the post office to open, then goes off to mail one envelope each to the ministers of war of six different world powers.

The postage is expensive, but noblesse oblige. Because this way, the six separate governments will be forced to confer and come to an agreement together to obtain a clear picture of the entire project. It's an excellent idea, in fact the only viable one, the sole way to make the plan work, except that the ministers will never reply.

28

TEN MORE YEARS LATER, Gregor is still waiting for the mail that failed to arrive either before or during the war, and only the pigeons are left. Not just those at home but those in Bryant Park as well, whom Gregor feeds after nightfall with old birdseed bought on sale.

Personally, I've had about enough of them, these pigeons. And you've had enough of them too, I can tell. We've had enough of them and to tell the truth, fickle and ungrateful things that they are, the pigeons themselves have had enough of Gregor. Tired of him and put off by the declining quality of his provisions, they have therefore decided to get rid of him.

The operation, highly organized, will take place one glacial winter evening. The nights fall early now, and Gregor leaves his hotel without greeting the elevator operator or concierge; in fact he hasn't greeted anyone for a long time. Few cars are in the street and very few pedestrians, because of the icy conditions. Scattered snowflakes are falling idly, inattentively, on Gregor's hat as he trudges toward the park, where the pigeons await him in silence, massed like commandos in the trees. As he waits across the street from the gates, absentmindedly watching the traffic before crossing, the pigeons spy in the distance, in the cold darkness, an automobile. It's an ancient, corroded Duesenberg, almost a wreck, its dirty-yellow wheels two-thirds deflated, its windows cracked and greasy, its convertible top in shreds, while confused memories of green or blue barely peek through the rust on the coachwork of the car. It's moving rather slowly but seems poorly under control, as if the driver were drunk, which he is.

When this car is almost abreast of Gregor, the pigeons suddenly flock to it, landing like shock troops all over its windshield where they pile up and spread their wings, like a thick and blinding blanket of dirty snow. Inside the car, the driver suddenly sees nothing, and without the time or the reflex or even the bright idea to use the windshield wipers, in his fright—heightened by alcohol—he gives the wheel an unfortunate turn: the Duesenberg lurches, skidding on the ice, and climbs the curb to knock Gregor down. Their crime committed, the pigeons immediately return to their trees as the driver, having swerved back into the street, zigzags away from the scene.

Gregor's hat has fallen off and come to rest above his head

but upside down, while its owner, unconscious on the sidewalk, lies alone in the freezing night and would probably die quickly from the cold, were it not for a providential policeman passing by on his rounds. He gets Gregor to his feet, tries to revive him, and covers him with his fur-lined coat while whistling madly for help. But hardly has Gregor begun to recover consciousness when he reacts brusquely, refuses an ambulance with a few blunt words, and without a single one of thanks, demands ungraciously to be taken straight to his hotel.

Back at the New Yorker, he won't allow himself to be seen to until he has summoned his errand boy to pick up the birdseed right away and dash off to Bryant Park in his place. A doctor then arrives, whom Gregor welcomes most rudely, insisting that he wear a mask and gloves to examine him. The diagnosis is three broken ribs, a cracked collarbone, and a depressed sternum; the prescription, three weeks of complete rest, but since Gregor has caught a serious chill, pneumonia turns those three weeks into more than three months.

One hundred days of solitude during which Gregor's mind sometimes wanders, and his fear of microbes grows so bad that he begs his rare visitors, even his rarer intimate friends, even Ethel, to stand farther away from him than ever—except for the errand boy, who reports to him every evening about his mission in the public squares and in front of Saint Patrick's Cathedral.

Although Gregor eventually recovers from the shock, his

health remains quite fragile. He has cardiac problems, the occasional fainting fit, and grows frailer, watched over by a maid
who comes daily to tidy his room. One morning, still in bed,
Gregor asks her, as she leaves, to hang the Do Not Disturb
sign on the knob outside his door. In spite of the ever-louder
screeching of the famished birds, panicking in their cages all
around his bed, three days pass before anyone will disobey his
instructions.